THE LADY OF THE MANSE

by

MARGARET NICOL

LONDON
PICKERING & INGLIS LTD.
1971

PICKERING & INGLIS LTD.
29 LUDGATE HILL, LONDON, E.C.4
26 BOTHWELL STREET, GLASGOW, C.2

ISBN 0 7208 2066 9

Printed in Great Britain by Northumberland Press Ltd.,
Gateshead, Co. Durham

To Love and to Cherish

1   MORAG FLEMING, WIFE OF THE LINNBRAE
minister, was busy stirring the soup in the Manse kitchen.
It was good, solid broth made with a knap bone, and
vegetables from the Manse garden, reinforced by barley
and peas. The good smell of it was wafted through the
big kitchen, which on ordinary days was the dining room
as well.

The real dining room, at the front of the house, was only
used for visitors and the other big room at the front was
also kept for state occasions. There were far too many
rooms in the Manse. It had been built in the days when
ministers had a large number of children. The Flemings
had only three: Brian, in his last year at school, Isabel
who was training for a nurse and young Andy who, unlike
his brother, was not gifted with brains.

Much as she loved her family, Mrs. Fleming was sometimes baffled by them. Not so long ago they had been such
helpless little mites utterly dependent on her. Now they
were huge; even Andy could top his mother by an inch—
and each was strongly individual. They might have been
other people's children, she sometimes thought, for all she
really knew them. However, they still depended on her for
bed and board and no doubt would appreciate today's
home-made broth. Packets and tins were all right at a
pinch, but there was nothing like the old-fashioned variety
for growing youth.

Everything was in the pot now except the parsley; she would have to take a trip out to the garden for it. Janet Bain, the daily help, was out there hanging up the dusters and other odds and ends. Janet was not an ordinary 'help', but more in the nature of a tradition. She went with the Manse, so to speak, and the Flemings had inherited her when they came to Linnbrae eight years ago.

If you could be patient with Janet's peculiar little ways, she was worth her weight in gold, so they had learned to live with her long-drawn-out tales, her strident outbursts of song and her utter scorn for labour-saving gadgets. She insisted on doing things the hard way, which worried Mrs. Fleming, for though Janet was tough, she was by no means young. How old she really was, Morag was to find out today for the first time.

It was one of those still, melancholy days that come in autumn when, if you took time to dream, memories of sad things would crowd in on you. But, at the moment, Mrs. Fleming had no time to dream. In her busy life, she seldom had.

She went down to the parsley bed, passing Mrs. Bain on the way. Taking a clothes pin out of her mouth, Janet remarked:

"Wouldn't be surprised if it rained. On my birthday, too!"

Stopping beside the sturdy, square-set little woman whose pink cheeks and dark eyes made her very pleasant to look at, Mrs. Fleming said:

"I didn't know it was your birthday, Janet. Why didn't you tell us?"

"Ach, you'd just have given me a present and I wouldn't have you go to the expense. All the same, I'll remind you when my next one comes round. It'll be my seventieth."

"You're sixty-nine, then? You must be joking!"

Janet was pleased. "Oh ay, I ken I don't look it. It's all this hard work that keeps me young. Would you believe that Tom and I will be married fifty years, come Saturday week?"

Morag certainly found it hard to believe. "I suppose you'll be celebrating. It's not every day one has a Golden Wedding."

Janet's cheerful face fell. "A celebration was in my mind, but Tom will have none of it."

That husband of hers was a strange man, as thrawn as they were made. How a cheery wee person like Janet had come to marry him Morag could not understand. It must have been the same sort of mysterious attraction that had drawn herself and Angus together. 'Most unsuitable', had been the general verdict then, yet no marriage could have been happier.

Janet and her Tom seemed to get on well enough, in spite of his crankiness. They had three sons, all living away from Linnbrae, and some grandchildren, too. Janet talked about them a lot, but it was difficult to follow who was who and Morag never interrupted to ask. Interruptions only made the story longer.

"Can't you talk him round?" she asked.

Janet pegged up the last dish towel before replying:

"I've tried everything. Tom Bain detests company. I thought when he retired he might join the bowling green or the Men's Own, but no. When he's not pottering round in the garden, he's away for one of his hikes, all alone."

It was true. Morag had seen him herself from the Manse window, plodding uphill with his stout stick and haversack, out for the day.

"He talks to the birds and the beasts," bemoaned Janet. "He says they're better company than humans."

"But surely—his own family—" put in the other.

"Makes no difference. The three boys have all written asking what we're doing about the wedding. Jamie—he's the eldest—is a baker, and he's offered to make us a cake. Tom and he never got on, and he won't hear of it. It's a fair scunner, that's what it is!" She blinked away a tear. Then, recovering, she went on: "I was wondering if the minister could possibly have a word with him?"

Janet belonged to the old school. To her the minister was a special being. His words were pearls of wisdom and he would naturally know how to cope with every situation. His wife, who had learned from experience that it was not always so, replied:

"Well, it's not exactly a church matter, Janet. Wouldn't your Tom resent it?"

"He might, from anyone else, but he has a great regard for the minister. Please, Mrs. Fleming, could you ask him to put in a wee word?"

"Very well," Morag promised doubtfully, "but husbands don't always do what their wives tell them, you know."

"It's me that kens that all right!" declared Janet.

Had either of the two women looked round during their conversation, they would have seen the minister at his study window gazing out at them.

Angus Fleming, now approaching fifty, his hair going grey at the temples, was a tall man with a lean face made unduly long by the length of his chin. His friends at college used to refer to him as 'Chinny' Fleming and still did so when they met him. Their sallies were greeted with a smile which illuminated his thoughtful grey eyes and made his whole face glow.

That smile was on his face now as he stood looking out at the woman who for twenty years had been his help-meet and inspiration. She hadn't changed a bit, he reflected, since their stormy courting days. She still had that trim figure, the quick, active movements of a girl; indeed she was still a girl at heart though over forty now. But she had mellowed; the years with their experiences both sad and glad had made her into—how did Wordsworth put it?

> 'A perfect woman, nobly planned,
> To warn, to comfort, and command.'

Morag would have been the first to deny the description. She had often lamented her shortcomings as a minister's wife, her unfitness for the position. From the first she had rebelled against the idea of marrying him, but something stronger than either of them had made it inevitable.

He had met her first when holidaying on an Hebridean island with his mother. He was just through college, his studies having been held up by war service. He had never had a serious friendship with a girl; he was rather afraid of girls and those he did take up with had never met with his mother's approval. Not that Morag had, either.

She was the brightest spark on the island, the life and soul of all the village activities. Even at her daily job behind the counter of her father's newspaper and 'fancy goods' shop, Morag MacEwan was so gay and alive that she infected all those who met her. She was so pretty, too, with that neat little figure, laughing blue eyes and soft hair that just missed being red—who could help falling in love with her?

The minister lingered at the window, lost in memories. How he had haunted that shop, buying things he did not need, just for the joy of hearing her voice, looking into her eyes. He went to all the affairs she took part in, but she was so popular with all the young men that he felt he hadn't a chance. He began to blame himself then, for falling in love with a girl who was so unlike his mental picture of an ideal wife, and decided it was better to forget her.

So he tried to avoid this disturbing creature, wandering alone 'mooning', his mother called it, along the lonely island roads. He saw much beauty there, but it did not still the yearning in his heart. Then one day he came face to face with Morag on the road, and she was alone, too, wheeling her bicycle with a punctured tyre. They were miles from home and he turned and walked back with her.

"Do you do this often—come out on your own?" he asked her. "It's so lonely, I wouldn't have thought—"

She became serious, for once.

"I've got to be alone sometimes, to think," she told him. "It's the only way to get to know yourself."

It was then he realised, to his joy, that she was not a girl just out for pleasure; but had he not guessed that all along! During the long walk home they conversed on all sorts of subjects, confiding to each other their inmost thoughts. Before the holiday came to an end, his mind was made up to ask her to marry him.

At this point in his remembering, Angus Fleming's hand went up to smooth his ruffled hair and his face became a little grim. For Morag had dashed his hopes by saying 'No', kindly but firmly. She wouldn't do for a minister's wife, she said. For one thing, she hadn't the education to

12

keep up with him; for another, she wasn't the type to settle down in a Manse being very circumspect for the rest of her life.

"I'd always be afraid I'd let you down, Angus. The prospect frightens me. I wouldn't know the first thing about being the lady of the Manse!"

"It would come," he pleaded. "My mother would put you right about things. My father was a minister, you know."

She made a wry face. "Angus, dear, I'm not afraid of you, but I am of your mother."

And that was that.

He had not given up hope, however. During the winter he wrote to her, receiving very short replies. Next summer he was back again on the island, this time alone. Again he haunted the MacEwans' shop, to find Morag little changed. His insight was deeper this year, however, and he observed that beneath the gay exterior there was a deep, womanly sympathy. She lent an ear not only to the young men's badinage, but to the tales of the old and the very young. Tottering feet were guided on their homeward way and weeping children were comforted with a 'sweetie', their bleeding knees bathed and bandaged. He fell more deeply in love than ever.

When the shop closed for the day, he was always there to escort Morag round the bay to her cottage home. He would never forget the magic of those evenings beside the summer sea. It was then that a link was forged between them that nothing could break, though Morag still held out, saying how little she knew about being a minister's wife.

"It's not what you know but what you are," he said, taking her in his arms. "And you do know the one thing needful, how to be kind. The people here all love you. The church people will love you, too."

Carried away, she gave in at last. Their way was not easy. His mother still had not come round to accepting her whole-heartedly after twenty years. When he took her from her island solitudes to the town Manse in a busy street she was bewildered and often homesick. His congregation would have preferred someone more mature and her slightest mistake was magnified out of all proportion. Yes, those first years had their problems, but her strength of character had won through.

Now in the village of Linnbrae she had come into her own. More at home with country people, she had a marvellous way of soothing out friction and giving encouragement. Angus Fleming would have been lost without her, for he himself was not the most tactful of beings. Her price, he mused, as he watched her now, was 'above rubies'. As always, the Bible had a word for it.

They had been without an organist for some time, and Mrs. Fleming had been playing for the services, though not very well, for it was a small pipe organ in which she was untutored. Tonight was choir practice night and it wasn't till she was going out that she brought up the subject of Janet Bain's Golden Wedding. The boys were studying in another room and Isabel was at the hospital, her homecomings being very erratic.

"Angus," began his wife as she pulled on her gloves—"in case I forget, will you be visiting the Bains some time soon?"

Book on knee he looked at her over his glasses.

"Well, I hadn't intended to. Why?"

"Mrs. Bain thinks you could talk her husband round

about their Golden Wedding," and she gave him the details of the story. His face grew even longer as he listened.

"My dear, I am no match for Tom Bain. Thrawn as he is, he can talk the hind leg off a donkey. He would probably ask me whose Golden Wedding it was—his or mine?'

She agreed. "Yes, and he would go on declaiming about 'the liberty of the individual'. But couldn't you try? Janet is such a good soul, and she had made up her mind for a celebration."

"She certainly deserves one," reflected her husband, worriedly. Then his brow cleared.

"Morag, why not try yourself? Tom would listen to you. You are so much better at persuasion than I—"

Mrs. Fleming smiled. She was always better at doing things he did not want to do himself, how like a man!

She replied doubtfully, "Well, if you're still in the same mind tomorrow, I might possibly—" Then popping her head back round the door, she added: "All the same, it isn't my job, you know! I'm only the minister's wife," and she ran off, leaving him chuckling.

Next afternoon Mrs. Fleming left her husband to his sermon and the two boys to their own devices. Andy, she guessed, would be on the hunt for 'Conkers' and Brian would probably get down to his books. Or poetry. He had started to write little bits of verse which his mother pronounced 'Very clever, very clever indeed', but to tell the truth she could not make head nor tail of them. They were either very deep or just plain nonsense; she trusted the former. Brian was due to take his A levels next spring. She hoped the poetry would not interfere, but it was too soon to worry about that.

The Bains' house was close at hand, as were most of the houses of the parishioners, except those in the new housing scheme and the outlying farms. To visit these Angus had an ancient car which Morag had learned to drive, but she usually preferred to walk. It was good for the figure and she had recently suspected a middle-aged spread. Angus said no, but then he always saw her through rose-coloured spectacles.

Though only a few miles from the busy town of Shelton, Linnbrae had preserved an old-world atmosphere and some of its houses were very picturesque. The Bains lived on the top flat of an old building that had an open staircase at the back and rather primitive amenities, but they were attached to the place and would not have accepted a new council house if offered it. In this they were firmly of the one mind.

And indeed Mrs. Bain had made a beautiful little home with plants on the window-sills, pictures all round the walls and brass ornaments twinkling on the mantelpiece. When she opened the door to the minister's wife, Morag explained:

"I'm sorry, the minister couldn't come himself, but perhaps I could have a word with Tom?"

Janet looked doubtful. "Well, Mrs. Fleming, you can always try, but Tom hasn't much opinion of womenfolk."

The other laughed. "So he pretends, but I don't believe it's true. Lead on, Janet!"

Janet opened the kitchen door. "It's Mrs. Fleming to see you, Tom!"

Her husband glowered across his newspaper. He did not rise; such politeness would never have occurred to him. He just said:

"Oh, ay?"

Janet shook her head. Her glance seemed to say, "There, what can you do with that?"

Morag sat down and signed for her to leave them. Then she addressed herself to Tom.

"I just came to congratulate you, Mr. Bain. What a splendid achievement, fifty years of marriage."

"Is it?" Tom grudgingly put down his paper.

"Certainly it is. It's years since we had a Golden Wedding in the village. I hope you're going to invite me and the minister?"

Tom blinked. "Invite you to what? If Janet's told you there's to be a party, she's havering. She knows I don't believe in such ongoings."

"But surely you'll stretch a point for once. There's no happier thing than a family get-together at such a time."

"Then they can get together somewhere else," grunted Tom, picking up his paper again.

Morag was not deterred. "You'll be disappointing a great many people, you know. Janet has been looking forward to having a celebration."

"I ken that fine, and she's been telling her friends. It was her that got you to come here, wasn't it?"

"Well, she did tell me that you weren't in favour and I thought if I put it to you, you might change your mind," said the minister's wife.

Tom bridled. "I am not one to change my mind, Mrs. Fleming, so you see, you've been wasting your time. Thanks for coming, but you needn't wait any longer."

Morag saw it was useless. She had got him in a wrong mood—if he ever was in anything else.

Janet came down the steps with her. "It's no more than I expected, Mrs. Fleming. Don't fash yourself, I'll get over it. Either that, or I'll go my own way. Do you think I should?"

"You mean, make your preparations and hold the party in spite of him? Bravo, Janet!"

"Would you do it, if it was Mr. Fleming?" enquired the other.

Morag pondered. "Well, I couldn't imagine him, but yes, Janet, I believe I would. Do you know what I think? When the day comes and Tom sees there's no help for it, he'll give in gracefully."

"I only hope you're right," said Janet.

Progress was reported at the Manse each day during the following week. Janet had got in touch with her sons and they were all coming with their families on Saturday afternoon, Jamie bringing the cake with him.

"I hinted that their Pa wasn't keen, but they all said to take no notice of him," Janet informed Mrs. Fleming. "You'll come to the cutting of the cake, you and the minister?"

"You can count on us," Morag promised.

On Friday, Janet was less cheerful.

"The cat's out of the bag!" she bemoaned.

"Oh dear, how did it happen?"

"Well, I was leaning out of the window telling Mrs. Mackellar downstairs all about it yesterday afternoon, when Tom came round the house. I'm certain he heard, but he never said a word. I waited for ructions, but they never came."

"Well, then," was the cheerful reply, "your troubles are over, Janet. Didn't I say he would accept the situation?"

"Ay," gloomed Janet, "but it's not like him, not like him at all."

When she arrived at the Manse on Saturday morning to give things a 'lick and a promise', she reported that Tom had still not opened his mouth on the subject; in fact, he seemed unusually mild.

"So it will be all right after all. Wouldn't it be fine, Mrs. Fleming, if he made it up with Jamie? The lad's really fond of him."

"I wouldn't be at all surprised," said the other.

On the way upstairs to dress for the occasion, Morag peeped into the study.

"You'll not forget to be ready about four o'clock, Angus?"

His mind on his sermon, "Ready for what, dear?" he asked.

"The Golden Wedding, of course! I told you Tom had practically given his consent to the celebrations. At least, he's doing nothing to prevent them."

"Good!" said the minister. "I'll be ready."

In the bedroom with its view up the hill to the moors, his wife decided to wear the blue suit which Angus said matched the colour of her eyes. Having taken a last look in the mirror, she happened to glance out of the window. Who was that tramping up the hill with a stout stick and haversack? Surely not Tom Bain! Another look convinced her that the gangling figure was most definitely Tom's. So, as he could not stop the celebrations, he was going to escape from them in his own throuther way. Poor Janet! She would be heartbroken.

Pity for Janet and anger with Tom made Morag take one of these quick decisions that often surprised her husband and family. She raced downstairs and out to the garage, started the car and in no time was speeding up the hill after Tom.

19

It did not take long to make up on him. When she stopped beside him and opened the car door, he gaped in surprise.

"Tom Bain, are you actually going to desert your wife on this day of all days?"

He hummed and hawed. "She does what she wants and I'm doing what I want," he mumbled.

"I am very fond of Janet," Morag went on. "I know how much she's been looking forward to this. Think, Tom, fifty years she's been a good wife to you. Do you remember that day in church when you were married?"

"Ay, of course I remember it."

"And the vows you made to love and cherish her?"

Shuffling his feet, "Well, I've done it, haven't I?"

"I'm not saying you haven't. I only say that to disappoint her like this isn't exactly loving, is it?"

For a moment he was tongue-tied, then he replied with a grunt:

"Ach, loving. I'm not a man to wear my heart on my sleeve!"

"Well," she pleaded, "please wear it there for once. Come on, Tom! Jump in and I'll take you back to Janet."

He hesitated and she thought he was going to comply. Then after taking one step, he drew back.

"Na, na, you're not getting round me like that! I'm going for my walk. I'll be back when the party's over and not a minute sooner," and he set off at a brisk trot, refusing to look back.

There was nothing to do but turn the car and go down again. Angus was at the Manse gate wondering what had come over her. When she explained, he squeezed her arm, advising her not to worry.

"Probably they'll get on better without Tom, you know."

"No doubt, but how can you have a wedding without a groom?" she lamented.

The sound of happy voices greeted them when Janet opened the door. Flushed and as pretty as a girl, she was dressed in a green silk frock with ruffles round the neck and sleeves. But her eyes were moist as she informed them dolefully:

"He went off, Mrs. Fleming, the minute the young ones arrived. Just said hello and goodbye."

"I know. I went after him, but it was no good. Cheer up, Janet! It's him that's the loser, not you."

The kitchen was absolutely crammed with people and food. On a loaded table, a splendid two-tiered wedding cake had pride of place. There were not enough chairs to go round, but two of the young folk sprang up, so that the minister and his wife could be seated. The silence that had fallen at their entry was soon dispelled and the tongues wagged freely again.

"We might as well start," announced Janet. "Minister, will you please say the grace?"

Angus rose to the occasion as always, giving thanks for the goodness and mercy which had followed the couple during the fifty years of their married life. Then everyone fell on the food, even Janet showing every sign of a hearty appetite and joking away with the rest of them. Morag had to admire her for the effort she was making, but it was a different story when it came to the cutting of the cake.

Jamie, the baker, made a short speech beforehand, saying it had always been his intention to do his parents 'proud' on their Golden Wedding day. He made no allusions to his father's absence; nobody did, for their mother's sake. Then he put the knife into Janet's hand and said:

"Here you are, Mother! It's time for you to cut the cake."

Janet took the knife and stood up, giving the company a shaky smile. Then, as she put out her hand towards the cake, she suddenly broke down and burst into tears.

"I canna do it!" she sobbed. "I canna cut the cake without your father! He was there beside me when we got married. His hand was over mine and we cut the cake together. He ought to be here ... I canna do it alone—"

Distressed, the family clustered round her with comforting words, hugging and kissing her. Morag looked helplessly at her husband, her eyes full of tears.

Then, in the midst of this disturbance, a gruff voice was suddenly heard to exclaim:

"What's all the row about?"

They looked up and there was Tom Bain at the door. A moment of tense silence ensued, then Janet held out her arms.

"Tom, you've come back!"

"Ay, I've come back. Have you finished your tea?"

"Not quite," she told him. "I was just going to cut the cake."

"Well," he enquired, "what's keeping you?"

"I was waiting for you to come and help me," said Janet.

Slowly Tom Bain came forward and while the family looked on, he put his big horny hand over his wife's and together they cut their Golden Wedding cake.

When the minister and his wife left, the real festivities

were just beginning. Jamie and his father were getting on famously and Janet was looking, and sounding, on top of the world. Saying farewell to Tom, Morag knew better than to refer to their conversation on the hill. But Tom, just to keep himself right, whispered gruffly:

"Mind you, Mrs. Fleming, you're no to think I came back just because you read that lecture."

"Of course not, Tom."

"It was because—" he cleared his throat—"because it looked like rain."

Morag glanced out to a clear sky and replied solemnly:

"Yes, Tom, it does look like rain. You were quite right to come back."

The Flemings went home arm in arm.

"Just what did you say to Tom up the hill?" the minister asked.

She told him, word for word.

"H'm. I could have said all that myself and it would have had no effect. What is it about you? I've still got to find out."

Morag just laughed and took his arm more firmly.

Hearts and Flowers

2   BETWEEN SPRING AND AUTUMN THERE WAS
always a lull in church activities and the lady of the Manse
got a chance to breathe. Then in no time the winter's work
was upon them, beginning with the harvest festival. It
was an occasion which Mrs. Fleming thoroughly enjoyed, though the work entailed always left her feeling
limp.

"Why do you do it, Mummy?" asked her daughter,
Isabel, on the Saturday before the event, as she helped her
to gather bunches of flowers from the Manse garden.
"You go slaving on, day after day, and never get any thanks
for it!"

Morag Fleming sniffed up the earthy fragrance of a
dew-laden chrysanthemum.

"I don't do it for thanks—what an idea! Besides, gathering a few flowers isn't slaving."

"Perhaps not, but it doesn't stop there. What about playing the organ and being president of the Woman's Guild,
besides being at everybody's beck and call every hour of
every day?"

Her tone was so indignant, Morag had to smile. Isabel
always adopted a protective attitude towards her mother.
Though only nineteen she was a very assured person with
a mind of her own. Sometimes she was inclined to be
'bossy', a very unfeminine trait which Morag hoped she
would lose.

In some ways, Isabel took after her grandmother, being tall and well built, with dark hair and cool grey eyes. The old lady had never shown much warmth towards her son's family; perhaps it was not in her nature to do so. Morag hoped that Isabel was not going to turn out like that, too. A woman without warmth was such an unlovable creature!

"Why do you do it?" her daughter repeated. "Your life is not your own. I couldn't stand it for one minute!"

"Wouldn't you?" asked Morag with a smile. "You wait till you fall in love and get married, you'll see things in a different light."

Isabel looked unbelieving.

"Or perhaps you're never going to marry?" Morag teased her.

"I may or may not," was the thoughtful reply. "Whatever I do, I'll certainly not marry a minister."

"Exactly what I once said myself."

"Then why didn't you stick to it?" demanded her daughter.

"If I had, you wouldn't be here today."

Leaving her to think that one out, Morag carried the flowers into the house, placing them in a pail of water till the afternoon. Isabel was a problem. She would have nothing to do with the local lads, had never taken up with boy-friends at all. Even the young doctors in the Shelton hospital where she worked got no hero worship from this young nurse. Surely it wasn't natural?

In the afternoon, Mrs. Fleming persuaded Isabel, who had a free week-end, to accompany her to the church to arrange the congregation's gifts of flowers and fruit. Young Andy was also a willing helper. He much preferred climbing steps and hammering in nails to settling down to

25

his lessons. As for seventeen-year-old Brian, he was shut up in his room presumably studying, though his mother suspected he was writing a new poem. She had noticed a certain dreamy look in his eyes at dinner time.

Saturday afternoon, of course, was a time when the minister must be left alone to revise his Sunday sermon, or even to rewrite it if the first version did not please him. His wife switched on the study fire before leaving. Otherwise, engaged in thought, he would sit there till he was stiff with cold without realising it. Then he would start a cough or get twinges of his lumbago. Oh, yes, the minister took some watching, but it had to be done in a way he wouldn't suspect.

No church had lovelier surroundings than the one in Linnbrae. To reach it from the Manse one walked across the glebe to a rustic bridge spanning the Linn burn. This picturesque stream was a feature of the village whence it ran down through a leafy glen, a favourite haunt for lovers.

Having reached the end of the bridge, Morag and Isabel made their way past some very old tombstones to the side entrance of the church, which took them into the chancel and thus to the vestry and anterooms.

A few members of the Woman's Guild had arrived before them and were gathered in the kitchen surrounded by masses of flowers, fruit and vegetables. There were also pots of jam and other home-made delicacies. Dozens of vases, strands of raffia and other paraphernalia were lying about in confusion.

"Oh, there you are, Mrs. Fleming. Isabel and Andy too, how nice!" Mrs. Craig, the session clerk's wife, looked round, beaming. She was a cheerful, bustling sort of person, rather easily upset and put out of her stride. Morag was very fond of her and indeed of all the Guild members. On the whole they got on well together but just occasionally trouble cropped up. There was nothing to indicate it today, but instinctively she scented something in the air.

"How are things getting on?" she asked.

"We haven't really started yet," replied Jean Craig. "I had such a job to get out. My nephew turned up for lunch, the one that's a divinity student. He's staying for the week-end. You remember him, Isabel? He was here before."

"Yes, I believe I do," replied the girl, showing no interest whatsoever.

"He said he'd come along to give us a hand. Oh, here he is now."

Peter Craig came slowly into the kitchen, a slight young man with a bunch of fair hair over his brow, and shy blue eyes. He looked half afraid of the company of women, as if he would like to turn and flee.

His aunt drew him forward.

"Come along, Peter, don't be shy! Here's Isabel Fleming; you two can get together. There's lots of heather here —what about putting a sprig or two on all the pews?"

He complied willingly and the two gathered up the heather, Isabel looking slightly resentful. It was so obvious that Mrs. Craig was throwing them together.

The Guild women set to work to arrange the flowers in vases. They had a newcomer with them today, a Mrs. Conway who had not long come to Linnbrae from Edinburgh. Unlike the others who had brought overalls, she was not dressed for the job and you could see them eyeing her smart suit and meticulous hair-do. But she certainly knew how to arrange flowers; her vases were a picture.

Morag could not help remarking, "You have a gift for

this sort of thing, Mrs. Conway."

"Well," replied the other, well pleased, "I've attended flower arrangement classes for years and you get the know-how. What colours to mix and so on. The mistakes I used to make!"

"The mistakes I still make," laughed Morag.

Seeing she was not needed in here, she went into the church to help Andy fix up some sheaves of corn on either side of the pulpit. Down there Isabel and Peter Craig were working with the heather, each in a different aisle. Not one word was passing between them. You would think Isabel might at least try to make the young man feel at home.

Morag was on her knees gathering up odds and ends from the pulpit floor, when she heard the voice of the session clerk's wife beside her.

'Mrs. Fleming, something will have to be done about that woman!"

She got to her feet. Mrs. Craig's face was flushed and angry.

"What woman, Jean?"

"Mrs. Conway. She's interfering with everything. The minute you left the kitchen, she yanked my flowers out of the vase I'd just arranged and said she'd show me how to do it."

"Oh dear," sighed the minister's wife. "But you were patient, Jean?"

"I was, though it took a bit of doing. But she's started on the other vases now, and everybody's not as patient as I am. It's not as if she was one of us, either."

"But she is one of us, now," she was reminded.

"Maybe, but it's manners to wait till you're asked. The others are seething in there. Meg Hastie just planked down her things and walked out. The rest will follow, take my word for it!"

It was one of those crises which Morag was often called upon to handle. She went back to the kitchen to find her valuable assistants standing idle in a corner glowering at the newcomer, who was happily rearranging the flower vases to her own liking. She turned round to smile at Morag.

"There, don't these look much better now? I'll just go on and do the rest."

To say 'please don't' would have been to offend her and perhaps lose her to the Guild. Yet if she wasn't stopped, there would be ructions.

"They're simply lovely, Mrs. Conway," Morag said sincerely. "I wish you'd tell me what to do about the flowers in the Manse. Could you possibly come across just now? It's time we got to know each other."

Mrs. Conway was torn in two. "I'd love to—though I don't like to desert a job."

"But you've done your bit. The others can carry on; they know what to do."

"We ought to," said one dryly. "We've been doing it for years."

So Mrs. Conway was safely escorted from the church and into the Manse. Morag had stopped feeling self-conscious about the lack of luxury in the big, bare rooms. Many of the parishioners had far more sumptuous houses than hers, but no hint of envy ever irked her, for she knew that what she had in love and contentment was worth far more than material possessions.

However, she was a bit ashamed of her ignorance when it came to arranging the flower vases in the hall and front rooms. Perhaps it wasn't so much ignorance as sheer lack of time. She would bring in some flowers, fetch a vase and start to fill it, when the phone would ring or someone come to the door. The flowers would be pushed into the vase anyhow. 'I'll sort them later,' she would say, but 'later' never came.

The vase which confronted them in the hall was typical.

"You see, Mrs. Conway, I don't know the first thing—"

"It's all right, I'll show you," said the other eagerly.

The vase was carried into the back kitchen. There, the mysteries of flower arranging were explained to Morag, how you had to have a 'shape' in your mind's eye before you started and cut your flower stems to suit, and that you must include 'pointed' material as well as flat material. It was all rather baffling and Morag was sure she would never remember half of it.

The result was marvellous. Having admired it, she infused a cup of tea and they sat down to drink it in the small sitting room at the back—the room most used except the kitchen. Mrs. Conway became quite talkative. Tall and slim, she had hair which had gone prematurely white and her eyes were dark and rather sad.

Morag seldom asked questions about the church people's private affairs but they confided in her nevertheless, and this newcomer was no exception. She was a widow, newly bereaved; her daughter was married in Canada and her son had gone to a job in London. She had come to stay in the country because of her love of flowers.

"But perhaps it was a mistake," she sighed. "I've come to the stage when it's difficult to make new friends."

Morag laid a sympathetic hand on hers. "You've started well, joining the church and the Guild. Have patience. The folk here are a bit reserved, but they'll come round all right."

"I feel I've got a friend in you, anyway," observed the other. "What a fortunate person you are to have your husband and family still with you. You haven't a minute to call your own, have you?"

"I often wish I had!" laughed Morag.

"I used to wish that, but now the days are so long, I'm sometimes desperate to know what to do to fill in the time."

An idea was hatching out in Morag's mind. "Mrs. Conway, I've just thought of a way. Why not start flower arrangement classes in the village?"

The dark eyes brightened. "You think people would come to them?"

"I'm sure they would. Perhaps we could manage to get the church hall. Keep it in mind, will you?"

"Most certainly! And you'll come to the classes yourself, Mrs. Fleming?"

"Yes, of course, I'll be glad to."

There, she had let herself in for another undertaking, she who was so busy. But it would be worth-while if it brought comfort and friendship to this lonely woman. As Angus often quoted—'To know all is to forgive all'. She would tell Mrs. Craig and her friends about Mrs. Conway's predicament and they would understand that her seeming officiousness sprang from her eagerness to make friends.

After her visitor had gone, Morag looked into the church and found the decorations practically completed. Very nice they looked, too. Peter Craig was still hanging round looking lost. Isabel seemed to have deserted him.

"She said she had some shopping to do," he explained. Really, the girl had no heart.

"Why did you leave the laddie high and dry, Isabel?" she asked her later.

Her daughter became very distant. "I had shopping to do. Anyhow, he had very little to say for himself. I haven't any time for boring young men."

"I'm sure he wouldn't be boring if you got to know him."

Isabel gave her a withering look. "Now, Mummy, you're as bad as his aunt, trying to pair us off. When I want a man friend I'll get one for myself. Meanwhile, I prefer to be left alone, thank you."

Chuckling, her mother replied, "If you're so choosey, you'll be left alone all right!"

But Isabel pretended not to hear.

Next morning Morag was up a little earlier than usual, for, on this important Sunday, everything had to go without a hitch. Janet Bain, the Manse 'help' did not come on Sundays, as she had enough to do in her own house before going to church. Janet had not missed a morning service for countless years, come rain, hail, or snow. Despite her age she still sang in the choir and it was her firm belief it couldn't get on without her.

One task that could not be escaped even on Sunday was the feeding of the family. Cereal instead of porridge this morning, eggs and brown bread and honey, toast and marmalade: it was all ready for them by nine o'clock, when Morag rang the big gong energetically, not stopping till she got a response.

Isabel came down first, yawning and unapproachable as usual. Tousle-headed Andy planked himself down, pouring milk and sugar lavishly over his cornflakes, while

Brian sat contemplating the breakfast table as if still in a dream.

The minister was last to appear. He came in slowly and Morag thought he looked a little pale. Andy stopped guiltily till the blessing was asked, than Morag said to her husband:

"Are you sure you're feeling all right, Angus?"

She might have known better. Nothing irked Angus Fleming more than being asked if he were 'all right'.

"I'm perfectly well, why shouldn't I be?" She knew by his tone that he was not well at all, but said no more. Andy did most of the talking. That boy could talk like a book about every subject under the sun, in spite of being so behind with his lessons.

"Oh, do be quiet, Andy," said his sister crossly. "Breakfast isn't the time for discussions. Besides, Dad's got a headache."

"Not at all," put in her father. "There's nothing wrong with me I tell you. Let the boy talk."

But when the meal was over, he half rose from his chair and suddenly sat down again, his face white.

They gazed at him in concern.

"Your lumbago again?" asked his wife.

"I'm afraid so. Must have got a draught yesterday. I put off the study fire; it was too hot."

"Oh, Angus! Well, never mind, Brian will help you up."

But it wasn't so easy. Her husband's muscles had locked and he simply could not straighten himself. You could see he was suffering agonies.

"Back to bed," ordered nurse Isabel.

"Yes, Angus," agreed his wife. "You've got your tablets and your electric blanket. A hot bottle, too. If it doesn't

33

ease, we'll send for Dr. Campbell."

He did not give in at once. "Impossible! Who will take the service?"

"We'll find some one. How could you climb the pulpit steps, let alone stand up to preach?"

He saw the sense of it at last and they got him upstairs to bed. The sweat was on his brow as he lay back.

"What a disgrace, to fail them on a harvest Sunday!" he moaned.

It was a new dilemma for the lady of the Manse. She set her mind to work to solve it.

"Angus, I've just thought of something. The Craigs' nephew is here for the week-end, the divinity student. I'm sure he would take the service," and she went straight to the phone.

Peter was brought to speak to her. On hearing the request he was at first reluctant, but Morag talked him round.

"It would be good practice for you, Peter!"

"Yes, at the congregation's expense. But since there's no other way, Mrs. Fleming, I'll do my best. So sorry about the minister. I'll be round to see him immediately."

Though they missed their own minister, the congregation quite understood the circumstances and gave young Peter Craig their close attention. From her place at the organ, Morag studied the young man's face and her heart warmed to him. He was nervous and unsure of himself, but there was an earnestness there which showed he had the real stuff of a preacher in him. All he needed was more confidence in himself and that would come through time, especially if he married the right kind of wife.

Yes, she thought, a girl like Isabel would suit him

admirably. Her assurance would give him the right backing, she would spur him on when required, give him plenty of advice and encouragement. But what was the use of arranging a future for Isabel, even in imagination? The girl would make her own future. Her mother only hoped it would not be a loveless one.

"Well," she remarked, as they crossed the bridge on the way back to the Manse, "that young man will make his mark some day. Don't you think so, Isabel?"

"I don't know, I'm sure," was the cool response. "He's so very young, you can't possibly tell."

"Not so young as he looks. Mrs. Craig was telling me that he gave up a good job to go in for the ministry. He deserves credit for that!"

They found the minister a little easier, but still in no condition to get up. He was anxious to know how his deputy had fared.

"Famously," reported his wife. "He gave us a nice little talk, rather than a sermon; simple but to the point. And you need not worry about the evening service, for he has promised to take that, too."

She had arranged to meet Peter at the church in the afternoon, to try over his choice of hymns on the organ. He was there waiting for her.

"Was I all right this morning?" he asked with disarming frankness.

"You were splendid. We all thought so."

"Isabel, too?" he enquired eagerly. So, as she suspected, he had a soft spot for her daughter.

"Isabel too," she replied firmly, for she could not disillusion him.

He flushed with pleasure. "That will give me courage for tonight."

There was very little time to spare, so Morag proceeded hurriedly to open the organ. It was then the accident happened. A hymn book was knocked over and as Peter stooped to pick it up, a vase of flowers followed. Unfortunately, it crashed just as Peter lifted his head and it struck him on the brow, smashing to smithereens on the floor. Good thing it was a Manse vase! But there was no time to think about that, for when the young man rose to his feet, blood was pouring from a cut on his forehead.

"Oh, how dreadful of me!" Morag exclaimed as he tried to stanch the flow with his handkerchief. "That looks bad. Come along to the Manse and we'll attend to it."

Taking his arm, she led him into the house and the first person they confronted was Isabel.

"Oh, good," exclaimed her mother. "Just see what my carelessness has done. I think you had better take charge, Isabel. You know what to do better than me."

Peter faltered, "I'm sorry to be a nuisance. It's nothing, really."

The girl took one look, then she was at his side, settling him on a chair while she fetched hot water and lint.

"M'm, it's quite deep," she commented. "Keep still, now. What a mess your hair's in! I'll have to snip off some of it."

With gentle fingers she parted the fair hair that hung over his brow. No touch could have been more tender, no glance more concerned. As she watched her snipping off the hair and bathing the wound, Morag smiled to herself. She had no need to worry about Isabel's womanly qualities. They were there in full measure, waiting to be roused by someone who needed her.

Instead of being unnerved by his accident, Peter Craig

seemed to have got new inspiration. Everyone was impressed by the way he conducted the service that evening. Though his sermon was only a short talk, as in the morning, his simple earnestness got through to the people and his theme 'loving thy neighbour' could not have been more apt.

All the same, Morag was thankful when the time came for the closing voluntary, for it had been a long day. As the last chord died away she gathered up her music to depart. Some of the Guild women had stayed by to take the vases into the kitchen, where they would be collected next day, and the flowers distributed to various invalids and old folk. Isabel was still around too, and Morag saw Peter Craig hurry to her side when he came out of the vestry. His aunt and Morag exchanged smiles.

"They make a fine pair, don't they?" whispered Jean Craig.

"Yes, but we'd better keep our thoughts to ourselves." Mrs. Fleming took her friend's arm. "I want to speak to you and the others, Jean, about Mrs. Conway."

To the few gathered in the kitchen, she explained the need to have patience with the newcomer, who was so much in need of friendship. She also told them about the proposed scheme to start flower arrangement classes.

"Who would be willing to join?" she asked.

Jean Craig was first to offer and the others followed. A day was fixed to make preliminary arrangements and at last she felt free to go back to the Manse. When she got there she sank into an armchair, utterly exhausted. Just a tiny rest, she told herself. But the door opened and Isabel came in to say:

"Mum, I hope you don't mind. I've asked Peter Craig for supper."

She got to her feet immediately. "That's all right, Isabel. I'll attend to things the minute I've seen your father."

The minister was still in bed, but he said he was much better and would be all right tomorrow.

"Have you had a busy day, dear?"

If she had started to tell him, it would have taken far too long. Besides, she hadn't the breath.

"Quite busy, but I wouldn't have missed it," she replied.

It was the way she felt about all her days.

A Credit to Linnbrae

3   A BIG HIGHLIGHT IN THE ANNALS OF LINNBRAE occurred in the late autumn of that year. The village went 'on the air'. The preparations began in the spring and the church and Manse were strongly featured in the programme.

Morag Fleming heard about it first from a member of the congregation, a Mrs. Bennett, who lived in a villa on the hill. Popular as the minister's wife was with the parishioners, there were one or two whom she found it difficult to get on with. Sylvia Bennett was one of them. She was the type whose word was law among a certain group, and whoever opposed her views was asking for trouble. As Morag had a mind of her own, she had met that trouble once or twice and her heart sank one day when she saw the lady coming purposefully up the Manse drive.

On opening the door, however, she was relieved to see that the caller's face wore a pleasant smile. She had not come to complain, it seemed. What was her mission, then?

"Do come in, Mrs. Bennett. Just shut your eyes to the untidiness. We're doing a bit of spring-cleaning."

Mrs. Bennett's appearance, not to mention her house, were always so immaculate, that Morag felt uneasy under her scrutiny. She was acutely conscious of that ragged finger-nail, the loose button on her cardigan, the fact that her house shoes were too comfortable for elegance: 'bachles', Janet Bain called them.

Mrs. Fleming took her visitor into the small sitting room at the back of the house. She had been indulging in a 'wee cuppa' and the teapot was still on the hearth.

"There's still a cup in it. Would you like it?"

"No, thank you, I had afternoon tea before I left." She spoke in a voice as prissy as her person. Mrs. Bennett's accent made more people than Morag squirm. It was very precise and 'la-di-da', so different from the warm, homely voices of the local people.

"I came to ask for help," she went on, settling into the armchair with the 'lugs'. "I thought you would be the best person to apply to. You've heard me speak of my brother-in-law, Hugh Bennett, who arranges programmes for the radio?" It would have been strange if she had not, for Sylvia Bennett boasted widely about her husband's brother who was, according to her, 'high up in the BBC'.

"Yes, I've heard of him, though I haven't met him."

"Well, there's every chance that you will," she replied. "They're planning to put Linnbrae on the air!"

"Really?" Morag could hardly believe it. "But a small place like this has no importance, surely."

"It's a typical Scottish village with a long history, he tells me."

"Oh, yes, my husband has made quite a research into that. He certainly could help, but how could I?"

"I'll tell you." No one so gracious as Sylvia when she was asking a favour. "Hugh phoned me to say he was paying a visit to the village next week and could I take him to see some of the more interesting folk who live here. I offered to introduce him to some of my own friends, but he says they aren't suitable. Imagine! He wants local people, like the blacksmith and the joiner and so on. And old folk who remember past days in the place. The kind of people I don't mix with at all."

"It's a pity," observed Morag. "You miss a lot, you know."

"Well, of course I've got no reason to know them, not like you. I wonder if you would do it for me? It would just mean one afternoon of your time."

Morag pondered. "To interview all the interesting folk in this village would take longer than that. However, I might try."

"Oh, thank you!" She beamed on her. "And he said he would want a sort of character sketch of each—occupation, age, and whether they'd be willing to broadcast—that sort of thing. Better have it ready before he comes, so that he'll know what to expect."

Morag had not reckoned on this. "That will take some time."

"You'll possibly be paid something. I'm sure you could do with the money." Mrs. Bennett sounded so patronising, Morag almost refused forthwith. On reflection, she decided it might be a worthwhile experience.

"They might even ask you to broadcast yourself," suggested the other.

Morag laughed. "Me? No thank you!"

"Well, I expect to do my bit. They'll need a 'narrator', Hugh says. I said I'd be willing to do it. I've a notion my voice would come over well on the wireless. I've had elocution lessons, you see."

Morag had her doubts, but surely Hugh Bennett knew what he was doing.

"I'll phone immediately," went on her visitor, "and tell

him you are taking on the job." And with that she rose to go.

Morag took her husband into her confidence that evening. He seemed quite interested. "I always thought our little church would make a good radio study. People ought to know more about its links with the past. I'll look forward to meeting Mr. Bennett."

"You don't mind if he asks you to broadcast, then?"

"Well, it would be something new."

"Good. I hope the other victims will be as keen!"

She lost no time in calling on the people she considered would be suitable, but difficulties loomed up immediately. The ones with the best stories to tell were dead against speaking into the microphone. One or two thought the whole idea ridiculous—dragging Linnbrae into the limelight like that. She was left with a handful of local worthies all eager to take part. Among them was the oldest inhabitant, 'Auntie Meg', a strong-minded old lady who kept the sweetie shop. She had so much to tell Morag about Linnbrae in the past and how much it had changed for the worse, that it took a whole afternoon to interview her alone.

The blacksmith was also a worthy subject, as was Peter Miller the farmer. Then there was the secretary of the 'Horticultural', and the local joiner with his fund of homely humour. When she had enough material, she wrote it all down and dispatched her findings to Mr. Bennett. He thanked her and made a date some time ahead to come and visit the Manse.

"Oh dear," said Sylvia Bennett when informed of this. "Why did he have to choose that day? I've got to go to town, can't put it off. Will you be all right alone?"

Morag said she would. In fact she was quite relieved that Sylvia would not be there to shake her confidence.

The Manse waited breathlessly for the appearance of this superior being from the BBC. They would have to ask him to tea, of course. Did such people have a special diet or would ordinary food suffice?

He arrived early on a Saturday afternoon. Morag saw the silver-grey car coming up the drive and went to greet him rather nervously. A man in his forties, she guessed, darkly handsome in a haggard kind of way, with a charming smile. She took to him at once.

"Well, Mrs. Fleming, this is extremely kind of you." He gave her a firm handshake. "I look forward to your telling me all about this picturesque little village of yours. I enjoyed your account very much. How well you know these people!"

"It's my business, and pleasure, to know them," she replied. "My husband is more acquaint than I am with the history of the place. He's in his study at the moment. Would you like to see him now or later?"

He said later would do, and they set off in his car to pay their visits.

It all went off very well. Hugh Bennett was able by his questions to bring out of his 'victims' the special points he needed, and by his sympathetic handling made a good impression even on the outspoken Auntie Meg. When, very late, they returned to the Manse, her escort said to Morag:

"A good beginning, I think. Next time, we'll do some tape-recordings on the spot. It's so much more natural than bringing folk to the studio. We'll be able to record some of the characteristic sounds of the village, too." He stopped the car and listened. Up in the high elms in the churchyard one could hear the hoarse calls of innumerable rooks. "Yes, that will give the atmosphere all right. We'll record the church bells, too, and the congregation singing. Could that be managed, do you think?"

Morag was sure it could.

"And of course someone will have to read the script, connecting the different items."

"The narrator," put in Morag.

"Quite right. Someone like yourself would be ideal."

That took her breath away. "Oh, no, Mr. Bennett, I'm sure I haven't the right kind of voice."

He laughed. "It has a nice Highland lilt. I have a keen ear for voices, Mrs. Fleming, and yours would come through splendidly. It is warm and sympathetic; that's the main thing in a broadcast like this."

Morag was blushing furiously. "It's kind of you to say so, but don't you think Mrs. Bennett would be a better narrator?"

"Sylvia? Now, what put that into your head?"

"Well, she told me she was prepared to do it."

"Perhaps she is," was the dry response, "but I am not prepared to let her. Her voice doesn't fit in with Linnbrae. It's so hard and metallic it would alienate listeners immediately."

"Oh, dear," sighed Morag, "I'd love to do the job, but I'm afraid she'd be annoyed!"

He gave her one of his attractive smiles. "Don't let that worry you. I'll explain my reasons to her. She'll see sense. You'll do it, then?"

Still doubtful, Morag said she would see what her husband thought about it.

She had left instructions about tea and it was all prepared in the big dining room with Isabel in charge. When Morag introduced Hugh Bennett to her daughter she saw admiration in his eyes and something like awe in hers. It wasn't every day the Manse entertained such an important person, and even Andy was tongue-tied at first. Brian said little, being in his usual reflective mood. The talk during tea was chiefly between the minister and their guest. In fact, it developed into a serious discussion with differing viewpoints that threatened to make the atmosphere tingle.

Angus Fleming was a peaceable man with an open mind, but when he was forced into an argument, especially in the matter of religion, he stood his ground firmly. It began by his sketching out the history of the church, which had been a monastic stronghold, he said, as far back as the sixth century. Since the Reformation a church had stood in that same spot, the present one dating back two hundred years.

"There have been many ups and downs since then," he went on, forgetting to drink his tea. "Perhaps the most unhappy period was in Covenanting times. One of our ministers had to flee from his pulpit. Secret meetings were held in the hills which you see from this window. In many cases, discovery meant death. These people suffered great hardships for their faith."

"They certainly had the courage of their convictions," agreed Hugh Bennett. "Folk just haven't got the same convictions nowadays."

"More's the pity," was the reply. "As a man who has been around, Mr. Bennett, what do you consider is the one big need of people today?"

The other observed that there could be different opinions about that. Reforms were needed, certainly, the useful application of scientific discovery, education, a fairer shareout of this world's goods—you could go on long enough—

"Yes, indeed," agreed the minister, "but fundamentally what the world needs is Salvation. Unless that comes about, civilisation is doomed."

Hugh Bennett went slightly pink. Morag thought, 'Oh, dear, Angus is going to lecture him. I wish he'd chosen a better time!'

"Your tea's getting cold, Angus," she reminded him.

He took not the slightest notice. "We're forgetting fast that people have souls to save. You do believe you have a soul?" he shot at the discomfited guest.

"I suppose I have," he said with an airy shrug.

"Of course. The soul is what distinguishes us from the brute beasts. You do agree?"

"Yes, of course. Certainly."

The minister's next words were unexpected. "You are enjoying the meal my wife has provided, I hope."

"Very much. She is an excellent cook."

"I know. We feed well in the Manse. No doubt you feed well, too. We need food for the body, but we also need it for the soul. 'Man shall not live by bread alone.' I presume you know your Bible, Mr. Bennett?"

With a half humorous glance at Morag, Hugh Bennett replied:

"Well, it's rather a long time since I actually read it."

The minister shook his head at him. "That's what I mean. That's what's gone wrong with us, why so many people are neurotic, insecure, wondering what life is all about."

"Well, what is it about?" asked the other lightly.

But Angus Fleming was deadly serious. "It's about getting our souls right with God."

The visitor made another attempt at lightness. "Easier said than done!"

Mr. Fleming leaned forward earnestly. "So many people don't even try! Life is too short to start thinking deeply. They think in terms of this life, forgetting that other eternal life. Jesus said: 'Whosoever believeth in me shall not perish.' It's the choice we are given. Believe in this life and you will only have this life. Believe in eternal things and you can have eternity."

Morag was rather sorry for their visitor. She felt it was time to cut in.

"Angus, dear, please drink your tea. You and Mr. Bennett can have your discussion another time."

Sighing, he took a sip of the cold tea. "Please could I have some hot stuff? Sorry, Mr. Bennett. I don't suppose you are open to conviction, anyway."

"I'm afraid not," he admitted. "I hate to hurt your feelings, Mr. Fleming, but what you have been saying doesn't seem to apply to the modern world at all."

The minister sat back, his expression sad. "The people of Sodom and Gomorrah probably thought the same."

"Yes, and look what happened to them," chirped up Andy who had been listening, all ears.

After the visitor had left, Morag and her daughter washed up the dishes together.

"I wish Daddy hadn't spoken to Mr. Bennett like that," declared Isabel. "He's such a nice man and it made him feel uncomfortable."

"I thought so, too," concurred her mother. "But don't blame your father. To him the other world is as immediate as this one. He can't help talking about it. You talk about your nursing, don't you? You can't expect him to bottle up what he feels so strongly about. He'd be denying his vocation if he did."

"I see what you mean," said the girl. "But why get on

to poor Mr. Bennett? He hadn't done him any harm."

"No, but he's the kind that would make light of religion and your father sensed that. The spark to kindle his flame! However, I'll warn him to ca' canny next time."

"I hope there is a next time," replied her daughter.

Isabel need not have worried. Hugh Bennett came back to the village several times until all the recordings for the programme were 'in the can'. On visiting the Manse again he showed a very charming side of himself and there were no more uncomfortable moments. Meanwhile, the village was seething with excitement about the broadcast. Feelings ran high. Some were offended because they had not been asked to take part, others took exception to the ones who had. You couldn't please everybody. The inevitable happened when Sylvia Bennett learned that the lady of the Manse had been chosen as narrator.

Meeting Morag in the village one day, she stopped, bristling.

"Is it true what I hear, that you are to be the narrator in the broadcast?"

"Quite true." By this time Morag was beginning to wish it weren't. "Mr. Bennett persuaded me."

"But you've never even had elocution lessons!"

"I know. He doesn't seem to think it matters."

"But he practically chose me to do it!" exclaimed the other. "You talked him round, I suppose."

"Indeed I did not! If you really want a part in this broadcast, Sylvia, I'm sure Mr. Bennett would find something for you to do."

"No, thank you," snipped the other. "From now on I wash my hands of the whole thing."

Washing her hands, however, did not mean keeping

silent about it. Out to make trouble, she began a rumour that the minister and his wife were monopolising the whole programme and the most deserving people were being left out. The broadcast was bound to be a failure. Nobody would listen to it. The critic on the *Shelton Gazette* would be sure to tear it to pieces. Linnbrae would be disgraced.

It was Jean Craig, the session clerk's wife, who told Morag about the rumours. "Of course sensible folk don't believe her, but she has her followers and if the programme fails, you'll get the blame, Morag! It's up to you to do your best."

"I can't do anything but be myself," was the reply.

Morag never knew how she got through the recording; only the support and reassurance of Mr. Bennett gave her the courage. She could hardly bear to listen to herself on the replay. That voice should never have been allowed to go out on the air! The broadcast would be a fiasco, Sylvia Bennett was right.

The full broadcast was to take place at the end of November; it seemed a long time to keep them all in suspense. As the time drew nearer, every day brought mounting tension.

"I'm sure I don't know how I'm going to sit through it," moaned Morag at breakfast one morning when she and Angus were having an extra cup after the family left. "I wish I'd never had anything to do with it! How do you feel, Angus?"

The minister admitted that he wished it were over. To speak to a congregation was one thing, to speak to the whole world was another.

Just then Morag got up to answer a knock at the back

door. It was Davie Steel the postman. "Good morning, Mrs. Fleming! Just one letter today, from Dumfries."

Davie never neglected to give them advance information. No doubt he was well aware the letter was from the minister's mother. There was no mistaking that large, angular handwriting.

"It's for 'Mr. and Mrs.' from your mother, Angus. Shall I read it out?"

He nodded and she began to read. The note was short and to the point. Mrs. Fleming was anxious to see her son and the grandchildren before the worst of the winter was on them. She proposed to come and listen to the broadcast with them. If it was not convenient, would they let her know by return? She hoped they were all well and the church prospering.

Morag felt rather guilty about not having issued an invitation before this. About twice a year old Mrs. Fleming came to visit them, and they usually spent a few days with her in the summer. On such occasions everything went smoothly on the surface, because Morag had learned to keep her feelings in check, but the truth was that she never felt at ease with her mother-in-law.

Too well she knew that the old lady had never approved of her son's marriage to an ignorant little Highland girl who knew nothing of the duties expected of her. Having been mistress of the Manse herself, she had her own ideas of what was what, and when Morag failed to toe the line, she would inevitably hear about it.

Nowadays, Morag seldom argued the point, for Angus's serene belief that all was well between them must not be shaken.

"Well, that fits in very well," said the minister smiling. "It will be nice having Mother with us at the broadcast."

Morag was not so sure. The ordeal of listening to the programme would be bad enough without the pungent criticisms of her mother-in-law. However, there was nothing she could do about it.

Then came a second knock at the door. This time it was Janet Bain, the Manse 'Treasure'. Since her Golden Wedding day, Janet had seemed younger than ever. Husband Tom had taken a turn to himself. He was less thrawn and it was easier to please him.

"Too good to last," observed Janet, "but might as well make hay while the sun shines!"

Morag broke the news about the expected visitor.

"Ah well, a visit from their Granny will be nice for the bairns."

Janet did not say it would be nice for the bairns' mother, for she was a woman who sensed every undercurrent. Nor was it 'nice' for herself, for she and old Mrs. Fleming held opposite views about housework. Janet was used to doing things her own way and the minister's wife never interfered, but his mother had no such compunctions. However, that did not keep her from doing out the spare bedroom with a will and carting the mattress outside for an airing. By the time the day arrived, the whole house was shining.

Grandma appeared in time for the midday meal on a Saturday. The whole family was there, scrubbed and polished and on their best behaviour. The boys had been prevailed on to get their hair cut and Isabel to wear one of her not-so-mini skirts. Mrs. Fleming sat very straight at the table, her searching grey eyes letting nothing pass, as she put them through their paces, starting with Brian who was sitting there in one of his dwams.

"You're very silent, Brian. Haven't you anything to say for yourself?"

The lad came to with a start. "Yes, of course, Grand-mamma," he replied politely.

"Are you getting on with your studies? I suppose you're going to be a minister like your father?"

The boy flushed. "No, I don't think so. I've no gifts that way. I—I think I'll be a writer. Books and poetry and things."

She smiled indulgently. "That's only a phase, Brian. It will pass."

"Oh, no, Gran," he protested. "It's been like that since I was wee."

"Well, I hope your parents don't encourage you in it. There's no sort of living in writing—especially poetry."

Her eyes turned to Andy, who was gulping his soup as if he hadn't seen food for a week. "And you, Andy. What is your future to be?"

Andy grinned at her. "Me? I'm going to the moon."

His questioner did not join in the laugh. "Tuts, that's all boys can think about these days!"

And then it was Isabel's turn. She and her grandmother usually got on very well together. The old lady saw herself young again in the serious-minded girl who always accepted her little homilies with a smile. She had thoroughly approved of her decision to take up nursing.

"But of course," she said now, "you'll be thinking of marriage some day."

"Oh, I don't know," reflected the girl. "I think I could have a good career in nursing."

"But, my dear, the best rôle for a woman is to help a man in HIS career."

With a smile, her grand-daughter replied, "Oh, Gran,

that's old-fashioned thinking nowadays!"

The other sighed and shook her head. "I'm sure I don't know what young folk are coming to." And she looked directly at Morag as if it were her fault.

The minister said cheerfully, "At least they can speak their minds, Mother, which wasn't the case when I was young."

Gran looked a little hurt. She did not like being rebuked.

Morag needed all her wits about her during the week-end, there were so many things to see to, so many pitfalls to avoid. At church next forenoon, their visitor renewed acquaintance with several of the parishioners she had met on former visits. Among them was Mrs. Bennett.

"Now, there's a woman who is a credit to the parish," she informed them at dinner. "Really go-ahead, the kind that gets things done. She has invited me for afternoon tea on Tuesday, Morag. Wants my ideas about redecorating her home."

Sylvia Bennett certainly knew how to ingratiate herself. Morag wondered if there might be some underlying motive in this invitation, but put the suspicion out of her mind. It sprang up again on Tuesday, however, when her mother-in-law came back from Mrs. Bennett's.

"Did you have a good time?" Morag asked her.

The other sat down, prepared to talk. "An excellent tea. She is a marvellous cook, her scones were a treat." She continued after a moment, "Mrs. Bennett was warning me, Morag, not to expect too much from the broadcast tomorrow. A hotch-potch affair she says, bound to be a disaster."

Her suspicions confirmed, Morag replied:

"Mrs. Bennett would like it to be a disaster, I know. If it is, she'll declare it's because she wasn't in it."

Very severely, "Now, Morag, that is a most uncharitable thought, not worthy of a minister's wife. She tells me you are to be the narrator, a part she was to have herself, until you persuaded her brother-in-law to give it to you. I don't know what made you think you could do it. Angus will be all right in his part, but you have had no practice in speaking."

"You forget I'm president of the Woman's Guild," put in Morag.

"Oh that. Anybody can do that! Now, Sylvia Bennett has a very cultured voice. No wonder she is peeved."

"I can't help it if she is," was the reply. "I didn't persuade Mr. Bennett, he persuaded me. If the thing is a disaster, he is the one to blame."

That it would be a disaster, Morag was now practically sure. That night she hardly slept. She was going to bring disgrace on the church and on the village. Perhaps they might even have to leave Linnbrae. She didn't want to leave; she loved the place and so did Angus. The family would get broken up and things would never be the same again. Her pillow was damp with tears.

In the morning things seemed a little brighter but as zero hour approached, her spirits fell to a new low. The programme was timed for eight o'clock; there would be few Linnbrae folk abroad this night! Everybody had made plans to listen in, in their own homes or with friends, so that they could discuss the programme as it proceeded.

In the Manse, the small sitting room seemed very full as they gathered there some time before the broadcast started. Angus had brought a book and sat with a finger in his place, looking quite calm and unperturbed. Isabel was taking the chance to manicure her nails and Andy to make paper darts, while Brian sat glowering at a theorem in his Geometry book. Morag pretended to darn a sock and Gran, very stiff in a straight-backed chair, plied her knitting needles busily.

All these activities stopped the moment the programme was announced.

"A village on a Hill," began the announcer. "Linnbrae, where past and present mingle, is the subject of tonight's 'Scotland' programme. The subject is introduced by the lady of the Manse, Mrs. Angus Fleming—"

Morag dug her fingers into her palms. A split second's pause, then a familiar sound came through, the cawing of the rooks in the elms. As it faded, her own voice was heard saying:

"Linnbrae is a place so old that the beginnings of its story are lost in the mists of time—"

Angus smiled broadly, Andy gave a little snigger, Isabel and Brian nodded encouragingly, but Gran sat on with a sphinx like expression on her face. No wonder, reflected Morag, no more enamoured of her own voice than Gran was.

Some of the villagers went on to tell their tales and then it was the minister's turn. No doubt about Angus's voice being the real thing! As he traced the history of the little church, his mother nodded approvingly and his wife felt a thrill of pride. Then they were in the church itself, with the congregation singing the 121st Psalm.

> 'I to the hills will lift mine eyes,
> From whence doth come mine aid.
> My safety cometh from the Lord,
> Who heav'n and earth hath made.'

It was not faultless singing—anything but! The tones

55

were rugged, as had been their forefathers in Covenanting days. Morag now took up the story again, telling about the village women at the start of the century; how, when their menfolk were out of work, they had started a laundering service, carrying the soiled linen from the big houses in town, to wash and bleach on the village green. It was here that 'Auntie Meg' came in with her memories, and even Gran had to chuckle at her dry Scots humour.

And so it went on, flashes from the past interspersed with activities of the present. The question posed through-out the programme was: would the encroachment of the town and the permissive ways of modern society swallow up the quiet village for ever?

With this question, the voice of Morag faded out. For a moment there was dead silence in the room, then Isabel came and threw her arms round her mother's neck.

"You were good! It was a lovely broadcast! I'm proud of you!"

"Yes," agreed her father. "You're a credit to Linnbrae, Morag."

"Mum, you're the greatest!" was Andy's comment, while Brian declared, "I didn't think you had it in you!"

It was kind of them to praise her, but it was just because they loved her, of course. What about the thousands of listeners who did not even know her? She wondered what the morning paper would say. "A good broadcast. Pity about the voice of the narrator!" She could almost see the words staring out at her. Sylvia Bennett would have her revenge, no doubt about that. Gran's verdict, for which they all waited, did not serve to cheer her.

"It might have been worse," she remarked dryly. "Angus did quite well and the church bells were good."

"And Mummy's part?" enquired Andy.

"I prefer not to say what I think about that."

She might as well have said it.

Sheer exhaustion, mental and physical, made Morag sleep soundly that night. She awoke with a sense of relief that the broadcast was over, but doubts immediately assailed her. If she could only get away to some quiet place and hide herself till all the critics had had their say. But it was impossible; she would have to stay right here and face the music.

Janet Bain appeared at the Manse promptly with the *Gazette*.

"You heard the broadcast?" Morag asked her fearfully.

"Sure thing," was the reply. "Them rooks in the trees, just like real! And the singing. I was sure I heard my own voice. Did you hear it, Mrs. Fleming?"

"Yes, Janet, I did." You couldn't not hear Janet when she was singing, even in a congregation.

"Wh-what did you think about the narrator's part?" Morag asked.

"It was all right, Mrs. Fleming, really it was." Her very earnestness made her feel it had not been all right at all.

"Would you like to read what the paper says?" enquired Janet.

Her limbs went weak. "I—I don't think so, Janet, not just now." Put off the evil moment as long as possible. But it wasn't to be long, after all, for old Mrs. Fleming had got up from her bed and suddenly appeared in the kitchen.

"Good morning, Janet. Is that the morning paper?"

Janet handed it over with, "You'll be wanting to read about the broadcast, I suppose."

Morag stood quaking while the page was found. Her

mother-in-law read the column in silence, her face never changing.

"Could I see it, please?" Morag asked faintly, unable to hold out any longer. Taking the paper she read:

"Linnbrae goes on the air. This was a programme which deserves top marks. Those who did not hear it missed something unique. Something came through in this programme which stirred every Scottish heart and we congratulate our neighbouring village on the high level they attained."

What followed was even more remarkable. "Special mention," it said, "must be made of the narrator. It was a happy thought to choose a woman for this part, one who was at home in Linnbrae and whose sympathies lay with its people. Mrs. Fleming's voice warmed the cockles of the heart. Its depth and sincerity will not easily be forgotten—"

Morag laid down the paper and sat down quickly, for the place was going round. Her husband looked into the room:

"What's going on here?"

"The paper ... read what it says," she quavered.

His smile broadened as he read. "There you are! Perhaps you'll believe me now that you're a credit to Linnbrae."

She shook her head. "Perhaps he's not a very good critic."

"He's an excellent critic and everybody who reads this will agree with him."

She smiled. "Sylvia Bennett won't."

"What does Sylvia Bennett matter? Her opinion doesn't count for anything." He turned to his mother, "Does it, Mamma?"

Looking her straight in the eyes he repeated:

"You agree this critic knows more than Sylvia Bennett does?"

"I agree that Morag did better than I thought," was all the old lady would concede.

A Very Special Effort

4   UP UNTIL NEW YEAR EVERYBODY HAD BEEN remarking on the mildness of the winter. "We'll pay for it," pronounced the gloomy ones and sure enough, January in Linnbrae turned out to be a cold, miserable month with everyone falling victims to colds and influenza. Wherever you went you met long faces and even the Manse folk gave way to the general depression.

The most cheerful person around the Manse these days was Janet Bain who turned up without fail every morning with her face beaming like a lamp, ready to fill the chilly silence with the sound of singing.

"You certainly don't allow the weather to get you down," remarked the lady of the Manse one Monday when the landscape was blotted out by a thick swirl of snow which followed the happed-up Janet into the back kitchen. "You must be frozen!"

"Ach," said the other, "we never died in winter yet. Once I get tore into the washing I'll be as warm as a pie."

But it wasn't so easy to get 'tore into' the washing. Everything was there—shirts, socks, vests, a couple of sheets and a vast number of odds and ends, ready for the tub. Only one thing was lacking—the water to wash them in. It simply wouldn't get hot.

"Ach well, I'll leave the things just now and get on with something else," decided Janet. Which she did, while

Morag worked away with the fire, getting it to 'draw'. However, it soon became apparent that no washing would be done that day. By the time the water was hot, it was too late.

Morag sighed. "Now, if we had a water heater and a washing machine, we wouldn't be at the mercy of a sulky old fire," she ventured to remark.

At once Janet was up in arms. "You wouldn't catch me ploutering away with a washing machine! Give me elbow grease and wash board every time! Tell me, Mrs. Fleming, you've seen plenty of washings hanging out in Linnbrae. Is there any one of them cleaner or whiter than the ones I do for you?"

Morag made haste to assure her that her washings were as the driven snow compared with these others.

"Yes, and it's not anybody's fancy soap powder either: it's these hands and the will to work," declared Janet. "You'll see what I mean tomorrow. Just leave these things to steep and I'll be round bright and early!" And she bustled away to make her man's dinner.

It wasn't the first time Morag had considered the advantages of a washing machine. No doubt the church committee could have been persuaded before this to supply one, but Janet had always been against it. She hated anything mechanical; even the vacuum cleaner was a menace; she would as soon get down on her knees with a brush and dustpan. So Morag had not pressed the point. In any case the church was always hard up for funds and washing machines were expensive.

The snow went off in the evening and everything began to freeze up. When it grew light next morning, Morag looked out to a fairy landscape. The bare branches of the elm trees in the glebe formed a delicate tracery against a blue sky and everything around was a pure, glistening white.

All very beautiful, but it had its disadvantages, even its disasters. Morag waited in vain for Janet to turn up to do the washing. Never before had she been so late. When at length a knock came to the back door, it was not Janet, but her husband Tom.

"She can't come," he began in his gruff way. "She's away to the hospital."

Seated on a kitchen chair, he told her the story. On her way down their outside stair Janet had slipped and broken her arm. The doctor had come and sent for the ambulance.

"She said to tell you she's sorry," added Tom. "Seemed worried about you having to do the washing."

That would be her first thought, poor Janet. "She's not to worry about a thing. You tell her that."

When Tom had gone there was nothing to do but get started with the washing. At first Morag rather enjoyed the rubbing and the rinsing and 'cawing' the handle of the wringer. But she had not Janet's stamina and there were so many things. A whole week's accumulation for five people. By the time she had them pegged out on the clothes-line, her back was sore and she was ready to drop.

That washing machine was an absolute necessity! Janet would not be able to cope for a long, long time and even if she got someone else to wash for her, they would expect a machine. Everybody wasn't like Janet!

Cold meat for the midday meal with fruit from a tin. "Sorry, Angus, there was no time to cook," and she told her husband about Janet's accident. He made a note in his diary—'Visit Janet in hospital.'

"Poor soul. You're going to miss her, Morag."

"I already have! Angus, you've got a meeting of the kirk session tonight. Do you think you could bring up the subject of a washing machine for the Manse?"

"A washing machine?" You would think she had asked for the moon.

"I don't know, Morag. I've an idea they would look on that as a luxury."

"A luxury!" she exclaimed. "That's because they're all men in your old session. Ask any one of them to tackle a big washing and they'd soon find out! For centuries we women have been slaves, suffering in silence—"

His eyebrows went up. "Dear, oh dear, these are strong words."

"Because I feel strongly. You will put it to them, Angus?"

He made another note in his diary. "All right, dear, if I get a chance. Now, just you take a nice long rest this afternoon."

A nice long rest when all these clothes had to be brought in, dried off and ironed. But she said nothing. Men just didn't understand.

Instead of going to bed early that night, Morag stayed up till the minister got back from the meeting. He came in looking extremely worried.

"Very grave news," he told her, flopping into an armchair. "The fabric of the church has been under survey and they've found dry rot. It will take hundreds of pounds to eradicate it."

Morag's heart sank. This on top of all the other problems seemed too much. Her heart went out to her man, who had been so anxious to keep the church out of debt and had pretty well succeeded up till now. It wasn't fair that a minister had to be bothered about ways and means.

63

Surely his sole function should be to look after the spiritual needs of his people? To do that properly demanded his whole attention and concentration.

She put an arm round his shoulder and laid her cheek on his hair. "Try not to worry, dear. The money will come in, you'll see." And she said not another word about the washing machine.

In a few days Janet was back home, her arm in plaster, but she had been ordered to rest and indeed her accident had been a great shock to her. Morag doubted if she would ever again be able to tackle the same amount of work. In the meantime, she would not hurt her feelings by engaging anyone else, so she carried on in the Manse alone with the occasional help of Isabel, when she was off duty.

If only she had that washing machine, she was sure she could manage, but she would not ask for one, now that the church was faced with such expense. So, when next Monday came around, she struggled with the wash again. It was heavier this week and she was right in the middle of it when the doorbell rang. It would! But it was only Jean Craig, the session clerk's wife and secretary of the Woman's Guild. As they were good friends, Morag was pleased to see her. She infused a cup of tea.

"I'm glad of the break," she told her.

"Morag, you look quite exhausted! It isn't fair that you haven't got a washing machine."

"To tell the truth I was going to ask for one, but with this dry rot in the church—"

"Yes, I know," said the other. "It's a calamity, isn't it? We've simply got to put our shoulders to the wheel. I really called about this 'Bring and Buy' sale the Guild's running, Morag. If we made it a full blown sale of work, it would always help to swell the funds."

Morag agreed, and they proceeded to put their heads together to have a cut and dried plan to present to the Guild at their next meeting.

To tell the truth, Morag Fleming couldn't think where she was going to get the time to help with a sale of work. Mrs. Conway's flower arrangement classes, though most interesting, took up a lot of time in themselves, not to mention the hours employed in trying to beautify the Manse with dried leaves and the few winter blooms she could obtain. The Guild was quite taxing and the organ and choir claimed a lot of her energies, too. Then, the minister took more looking after than most husbands. He was always coming to her with little jobs to do; no wonder her days were so full. Nevertheless, there was always time for one more task, if you were really keen to fit it in.

The 'Bring and Buy' had been scheduled for a Saturday at the beginning of February. Keeping the same date, they enlarged the scope to include 'jumbles', a provision stall and a work stall for small items such as aprons and hand-kerchiefs. Morag said she would take charge of the 'afternoon teas', and when she mentioned the project to the family, Andy begged to be allowed to preside at the 'White Elephant' stall. As for Brian, he agreed to take charge of a second-hand bookstall. Isabel, when appealed to, begged to be excused.

"I don't even know if I'll be off that afternoon, Mum, but if I am, I promise to support you all," she declared.

From the start that 'special effort' went with a swing. It was often like that with things got up in a hurry; there wasn't time for snags to arise and enthusiasm to ebb.

For a wonder the weather was mild and sunny and

people who had been incarcerated all winter had the courage to venture out of doors. Morag was glad she had taken on the teas, for she got a chance to speak to folk she had not seen for a long time.

Quite a stir was caused when Janet Bain, broken arm and all, sat herself at a table declaring that she would be served by no one but the lady of the Manse.

Morag hurried to her side. "Lovely to see you out, Janet! How are you feeling?"

"Just fine, Mrs. Fleming. Raring to go, in fact, if it wasn't for this gammy arm. How are you getting on with the washings? Not sending to the laundry, I hope?"

"No, I haven't sunk as low as that yet," laughed Morag. "Besides, it's too expensive. I manage, but the things are not whiter than white any longer, I'm afraid."

Janet was gloomy. "You haven't got the strength in these wee wrists. I never thought to see a washing machine in the Manse, but it might have to be."

"Not in the meantime, Janet. It's this dry rot. The church is more important than the Manse."

"Why should it be?" demanded Janet. "Get some womenfolk on to the session and it would be a different story."

"Wheesht," warned Morag. "Do you want the wrath of heaven to descend on us?"

Having attended to Janet's needs, she turned to another table. To her surprise it was her own daughter who was sitting there: Isabel, looking very bonnie, with an unwonted sparkle in her grey eyes. Nor was she alone. Her companion was Hugh Bennett. These two seemed to be very friendly, though to Morag's knowledge they had not met since the important occasion when Linnbrae went 'on the air'. Perhaps Isabel had met him since in

66

Shelton, and had not mentioned the fact.

Morag gave Hugh Bennett a quick, appraising glance before speaking. In early middle age, with hair streaked with grey, and dark eyes that were somewhat tragic, he was just the kind of man to appeal to a young girl who had little time for lads of her own age.

He looked up, politely standing to greet her.

"Hello, Mrs. Fleming! Pleased to meet our distinguished 'narrator' again."

Morag smiled. "You were very kind to us, Mr. Bennett, about that broadcast. Now, what can I get you? Some nice home-made sausage rolls?"

"That for me too, Mummy," declared Isabel, whose cheeks were attractively pink. "Is everything going all right?"

"Oh, yes, the money's pouring in," and Morag went to the kitchen to get their order. Mrs. Craig was in there cadging a cup of tea and taking a break from her provision stall.

"I see Isabel has a new boy-friend," she observed confidentially. "I'm so disappointed. I was hoping that she and my nephew Peter—"

"So was I," Morag told her. "But surely there's nothing in this, Jean. Isn't Hugh Bennett a married man?"

"Not now," was the whispered reply. "Haven't you heard about him? His wife left him several years ago. Poor man, he's been through a lot. She died later without being reconciled. They say he's never got over it."

"I see. How sad."

She could see how such a man would be able to evoke her daughter's deep sympathy, to the extent, perhaps, of her falling in love with him. If it so happened, like many another mother, she would probably be helpless to avert it.

But no doubt she was worrying about nothing. Taking a plate of sausage rolls from the oven, she got on with her duties. One thing at a time. There were enough present problems to face without creating imaginary ones.

The money had poured in sure enough. Next day the minister announced from the pulpit that the Guild sale of work had made well over a hundred pounds, with donations. It was quite a triumph and when the ladies gathered for their Wednesday afternoon meeting, they all looked very pleased with themselves.

The chief item on the programme that day was the yearly 'allocation of funds', when their assets were added up and donations earmarked for different causes. Mrs. Fleming was in the chair as usual and Jean Craig as secretary-treasurer stood at the blackboard, chalk in hand, to total up the sums.

Missionary causes, convalescent homes and such like were accorded their customary gifts. When it came to the big sum which had been made by the sale of work, Mrs. Fleming got up to announce:

"I have no doubt that everyone will agree that the whole of this sum should go to the church fabric fund, to help with the problem of dry rot. Are there any objections?"

To her surprise, Jean Craig turned to the meeting.

"Ladies, before we decide on this step, I'd like to make another proposal. It's about the Manse. Mrs. Fleming has been battling for a long time with out-of-date equipment. She is now coping unaided with big washings every week and there isn't even a washing machine.

"I think it's shameful, ladies, that we should allow this to go on, so I propose that the price of a washing machine should be deducted, before we hand over these proceeds to the fabric fund."

Morag smiled at her in grateful bewilderment as murmurs of assent came from the meeting.

"I can see that my suggestion has your approval," went on Mrs. Craig. "Perhaps we can have a show of hands?"

Before she could go any further, however, one of her listeners sprang to her feet.

"Mrs. Craig, I must beg to disagree!"

Morag groaned silently. It was Mrs. Bennett, her bête noire. The lady's attendances were few and far between, but she had to be here today, of course.

"It was understood by everybody," declared Sylvia Bennett, "that this effort was solely for the fabric fund, which is a much more crying need than a mere washing machine."

'Depend on it,' thought Morag, 'she has a washing machine herself and a spin dryer, too!'

But the speaker had not yet finished. "This large sum," she went on, "will give a great boost to the fund and to the Guild as well. Think of it—how many Woman's Guilds could give such a handsome donation? It will reflect great credit on us, not only locally. We want to give our cause new heart, don't we?"

Morag could see she had made an impression, especially among her own particular adherents. She rose from her seat.

"Ladies, I'll leave you to talk this matter out. You will feel more free if I am not here."

She went into the kitchen and closed the door. To be or not to be? She certainly did not want a washing machine

69

against opposition. Jean Craig would have carried them if it hadn't been for that woman. "But I must not think of her as 'that woman'. Angus would be horrified."

At last Jean Craig opened the door. "Will you come in now, Mrs. Fleming?"

Dead silence reigned as she took her seat. "The position is this," the secretary went on, "after a show of hands, the voting is even. As chairman, you have the casting vote. So it remains with you."

Was ever the lady of the Manse faced with such a dilemma? But there was only one answer for Morag.

"Then, of course," she replied, "I vote that the money, all of it, should go to the fabric fund."

Jean Craig was angry. Angry with Mrs. Bennett but annoyed with Morag, too.

"I can't understand you," she told her afterwards. "It was your big chance. I'm sure they're sorry already that they listened to the Bennett woman. What's the good of me trying to help you if you won't help yourself?"

Morag took her arm placatingly. "It wouldn't have done, Jean. I'd never have enjoyed using a washing machine gained by a casting vote! No, I'd rather go on rub-a-dubbing."

And that was what it would be ad infinitum, she told herself on the way back to the Manse.

Brian was home from school, lolling in the sitting room reading a magazine. He gave quite a start when she spoke.

"Hello, all alone? Andy not home yet?"

He thrust the magazine out of sight. "No, not yet. He wasn't on the bus."

"Oh, dear, he must have been kept in again. He was

late three nights last week. I think your father had better go and see the headmaster."

"Oh, no, there's no need for that, Mum," was the quick reply. "Please don't fuss. Andy's all right."

"All right? He's getting worse at his lessons instead of better!"

The Head had told them Andy was a 'late developer' and they should have patience; but they had waited and waited and nothing had happened. "Couldn't you help him with his lessons, Brian?"

"I could," said the boy, "but he simply won't let me. Why worry about Andy? He's not clever, but everybody likes him."

"I suppose he's what's called an extrovert," sighed Morag. "What's that magazine you were reading, Brian?"

"This?" He flushed. "Oh, it's just a poetry magazine. It wouldn't interest you, Mum. You're not poetically inclined, are you?"

"I suppose not." Poetry and she were far apart. A regular Martha she was these days, though her rôle sometimes changed, when she and her husband were alone together and he read to her from the Bible or the classics. To give complete satisfaction, perhaps a minister's wife had to be both a Martha and a Mary; a worker and a listener as well.

Andy came in at last in the middle of the evening meal. He answered questions so vaguely that his mother was annoyed. Isabel did not turn up at all, but when the meal was over, the phone bell rang in the hall.

"It's me, Mummy," came Isabel's voice. "I'm sorry, but I won't be home till late."

"What a pity, dear. They're working you very hard in hospital, aren't they?"

"Well," was the reluctant reply, "it's not exactly work. I'm going out with somebody."

If she asked who the 'somebody' was, Isabel might resent it, but she did not need to ask. Something told her it was Hugh Bennett. But she only said:

"Very well, dear. Don't be too late, will you?"

Not for the first time, she wondered if she had somehow failed as a mother. Some of her friends boasted that their young ones 'told them everything'. Hers kept themselves very much to themselves. Even Angus was a bit distant this weather; it was probably due to all that worry about the church. Oh, well, she supposed there was only one thing for her to do, and that was to keep on loving them, whatever happened.

Monday again and another big washing to face. She was rather short with them all at breakfast that morning, giving Brian a scolding for dreaming and Andy for spilling the milk. Isabel was told off for having an untidy bedroom and altogether the atmosphere was a bit strained.

Then, after they had gone and Angus had kindly helped her with the dishes, rushing off to his study in case he was asked to do something else (or so she imagined) she started on the long, arduous job of 'rub-a-dubbing', which seemed this morning to be more tiring than ever.

For practically the first time in her life Morag began to feel sorry for herself. 'It's not fair,' she thought. 'It's simply not fair! It wouldn't be so bad if the family cared, but not one of them realises what I do for them. They think I'm a sort of tireless automaton without any feelings.' A few tears were mixed with the soapsuds. Then, just as the first batch was ready to hang out, the rain came down in torrents.

It was the last straw. She sat down, defeated, and had what Janet called 'a good greet'.

The flood was stemmed by a knock at the back door. Dabbing her eyes quickly, she opened it. Two hefty men were there in charge of—was she seeing straight? Yes, there could be no doubt about it—a sparkling new washing machine!

"Oh, but that can't be for me," gasped Morag.

"It's for the Manse," they declared. "Will you sign for it, please? Somebody will be here tomorrow to fix it up for you."

Dazed, she indicated a corner of the back kitchen and they lifted it in. Then with grins and good wishes they went away and Mrs. Fleming was left standing over the new possession, laughing and crying at the same time. Where had it come from? That was the mystery.

Perhaps Angus knew something. In two ticks she was upstairs, bursting into the study.

"Angus, Angus, a washing machine!"

He stopped writing and stood up smiling. "So it has come. It's late. I meant you to have it for today's wash."

"You—you bought it yourself? But Angus, you couldn't afford it!"

"Not alone." He had put his arm round her and was looking with love into her eyes. "The children helped. Brian won a poetry competition. His poem's in the magazine but he didn't want you to guess, yet. Isabel contributed her savings and Andy—well, I don't know if he was within his rights or not, but he has been carrying luggage at Shelton station and getting tips—"

"Trust Andy," gasped his wife.

He bent down from his tall height to kiss her. "Yes,

73

Morag, trust them all. They love you; they won't let you down."

"No, Angus." Her voice was chokey. "Oh, I'm so happy!"

"Because you've got a washing machine?" he asked.

"Because of the people who gave me it," she replied.

———

A Hope for the Future

5   Linnbrae church was well-off in having a fairly new pipe organ with fine possibilities. The trouble was that Mrs. Fleming, when she took over the duty of organist, knew very little about the instrument. She had always meant to take lessons but never found time, even if there had been anyone to teach her.

In any case they were always hoping to get someone else to take on the organ, but though they advertised periodically, no one suitable came forward.

So there was the lady of the Manse seated at the organ one Friday night, trying to get the music out of it that she knew it was capable of, but failing sadly. It was choir practice night and while the members gathered she was taking the chance to get in a little organ practice too.

Possibly the folk in the choir were quite satisfied with what they heard, but she was not. She knew what real organ music could sound like; it charmed the ears, but it did much more. It carried one away; it lifted the heart up to heaven. She would never forget a certain organ recital she had listened to with her husband in a church in Shelton a few years ago.

An organ recital ... Now, if they could get someone to come and give them an organ recital here, it would not only serve to bring out the best in their organ, it would be one more boost to the fund that everyone was working for. The sooner the dry rot in the church was attended to, the less it would cost; therefore, it was all shoulders to the wheel.

They were all there now in the choir; at least, all that were coming. A nice crowd of people, a real cross section of the church membership. In age they ranged from a few young girls in their teens to Janet Bain, who was nearly seventy. More women than men, of course, it was always the way. And only two tenors. However, Jo Finlay the banker and wee Sammy Steel the painter were staunch adherents who never let her down.

All they had to do tonight was to try over the hymns for Sunday plus a fairly easy anthem. Still absorbed in the new idea of an organ recital, Morag let them carry on, except when they actually sang wrong notes or Janet Bain's enthusiasm ran away with her. Recently, the strength Janet lacked in her broken arm seemed to have gone into her voice. But she took Mrs. Fleming's hints with a good grace, though by Sunday she would probably have forgotten them again.

The practice over, Morag pushed in the organ stops, closed the lid and descended from her perch.

Janet Bain was waiting to speak to her.

"I heard you had a washing machine in the Manse," she began.

Morag felt quite guilty. "Yes, Janet. Don't be angry! When you're able to come back to help, you will find it a great boon."

"Maybe aye and maybe hooch aye," observed Janet, "but I won't deny you're better with it, as things are. Mrs. Fleming, I'm champing at the bit. I'm sure there's something a one-armed bandit like me could do for you in the Manse. Can I come tomorrow for a couple of hours?"

Morag had been waiting for such a suggestion. She

knew that idleness did not agree with Mrs. Bain.

"Come by all means, if you're sure you're fit."

"Never fitter. Raring to go, that's me!"

It would be quite a relief to be under Janet's sway again, though her critical eye would doubtless find many details that had not been attended to. The truth was that Morag had just been putting a 'face' on things since Janet's accident. Not that anyone had complained. Neither Angus nor the boys would have noticed a whit wrong if a cyclone had hit the house. Even Isabel, hygiene mad as she was, had found no fault. But Isabel had not been herself lately. Very quiet, very mild, away up in the clouds; she had all the symptoms of a girl in love.

The door opened and Janet said, "Here's the minister come to fetch you."

It was Angus Fleming's habit to look in at the end of the choir practice to have a word with the members and escort his wife back to the Manse, past the tombstones and over the bridge. It was an eerie walk on a winter's night.

When good nights had been said, Morag took his arm and they strolled slowly along under the moon, feeling very close together.

"How did it go tonight?" he asked.

"Much as usual. Janet Bain's coming back tomorrow to help out, Angus."

"I'm relieved to hear that."

"Yes, you'll get off with the breakfast dishes now." She switched to the matter which had been in her thoughts. "Angus, I've just had an idea."

He was used to those ideas of hers and had learned to take them calmly.

"What is it this time?"

"You remember that organ recital we went to in Shelton? The organist was Gavin Robertson."

"I do," he replied, "and I also remember the shameless way you went up to him afterwards and kept him talking, without an introduction even."

She laughed. "I didn't need an introduction. I knew that he came from the Island, same as me, and that made a link between us." For her there was only one island and all who belonged there were akin. She went on, "He was a wonderful organist, wasn't he? And such a nice man. Do you think if we invited him here he would give us a recital in aid of the funds?"

The minister thought it over, as he did everything. "We could always enquire, I suppose, but he may have forgotten all about you."

"Yes, he may, but I can remind him, can't I?" She pressed his arm coaxingly. "You know the minister of his church, Angus. Will you phone him tomorrow and ask him how we can get in touch?"

"Yes, well, I'll have a word with him about it." She knew his tone of voice meant, "Since you ask I can't refuse, but please try not to make any more requests." She did not blame him, for he had so many demands on his time and patience. Though naturally the most obliging of beings, he'd had to build up a certain resistance. It was a lesson she had never learned herself.

Janet turned up at her usual time next day and got 'tore in', as she expressed it. It turned out that she could do marvels with her left hand even to sweeping the floor and polishing the furniture. It left Morag free to tidy out drawers and defrost the 'fridge, but she did not forget about her husband's promise to phone the minister in Shelton.

Getting the number for him, she thrust the phone into his hand, then rushed to the back door to buy a string of onions from the Breton onion seller, who always loved a chat. When she came back Angus was standing in the hall looking very grave.

"Well, did you get him? What did he say?" she asked.

"It's a sad little tale, Morag. I'm afraid you'll have to give up your big idea. Gavin Robertson retired a year ago. He has given up playing altogether."

Disappointed, "Oh, dear, what a pity, he was so gifted! Did the minister say why he had given up?"

"He did, that's what makes it so sad. He lost his wife, then he had a serious illness. It left him without his sight and with no interest in life whatever."

Morag was stricken with compassion. In her capacity as wife of a parish minister she had come in contact with much trouble. There was so much suffering in the world, borne by so many blameless people, it had sometimes baffled her. It was Angus, who had pointed out the one bright aspect; the ability of the human spirit, strengthened by faith in God, to overcome. She had seen it happen time and again. The brightest people were often those who had the most to bear. Their courage was an inspiration to all who knew them.

She could not get the thought of Gavin Robertson out of her head. He was not an old man—in his late fifties, she would say. She remembered his face well, especially the luminous grey eyes which shone so kindly upon her when she spoke about the island he had left when a boy. To think of those eyes being sightless, his mind overburdened by illness and loss. Music to him must now seem a mockery.

From her girlhood on the island when she was in charge

of her father's shop, Morag's impulses had always been not only to pity, but to help those in trouble. It was this quality that Angus Fleming had sensed long ago in the light-hearted girl who seemed to laugh her way through life. Unsuitable, some said, for a minister's wife, she yet had the one thing needful.

So Morag, true to form, began to wonder if there was any way she could bring some kind of comfort to the stricken man. And of course there was. She could go and see him and talk about their island. In his blindness the eye of memory would still be sharp and clear.

This very afternoon she had some shopping to do in Shelton. To find Gavin Robertson's address was easy; it was there in the telephone directory. In case she turned coward on the doorstep, she said nothing of her intentions. Getting off the bus at the Square, she made her way to Sutherland Avenue, a street of solid stone houses built in spacious Victorian days. At number 17 a brass plate with his name and music degrees showed that Gavin Robertson still lived there.

She looked up at the big silent windows which seemed to be asking her what she was doing there, but she pulled the bell and waited, feet firmly planted. Footsteps now, and then the door opened to reveal a young woman with smooth dark hair and black-lashed grey eyes, so like those other eyes there could be no doubt about her identity.

"Miss Robertson?" faltered Morag, and went on to explain who she was. "We phoned your minister to ask if Mr. Robertson would give us an organ recital, and were told about his illness. I feel so sorry—"

The door was opened wide and she was taken into a room even bigger than the Manse rooms, with leather upholstered furniture, and massive pictures on the walls.
80

"I'm afraid you will find my father sadly changed," said Ruth Robertson. Her small face was very pale and you could see that she had been through a lot. On the slim finger clasped on her lap, Morag noticed a diamond engagement ring. "He's having his afternoon rest now," she went on. "Though he is better physically, he's in such a state of depression nothing will rouse him. For days he just sits and mopes, won't go out even, and doesn't try to help himself at all. I try to get him to learn Braille or apply for those talking books that are such a godsend, but he seems set against anything that needs the slightest effort."

"He must feel absolutely hopeless," said Morag. "All this is very hard on you. Are you all alone with him?"

"Except for the housekeeper, but he clings to me, so I never leave him. I'm all he's got left ... When he took ill," she went on, twisting her ring with a wistful smile, "I was about to be married, but of course that had to be put off. He's been a good father to me and now that he needs me so much I can only devote my life to him." It seemed to be a relief to her to talk.

Morag realised that this girl was one of those unsung heroines of whom she had met not a few, who give up all their hopes for parents who need them, and who sometimes receive little thanks.

Ruth got to her feet as a tremulous voice was heard calling her name.

"I'll see if my father wants to talk to you, but please don't be surprised if he prefers not to."

She left the room to return with her father leaning on her arm. Morag was shocked to see the ravaged face and bowed figure of the man she remembered at the height of his powers. She clasped his hand warmly.

"Mr. Robertson, do you remember me? Morag Fleming,

the Linnbrae minister's wife. I met you at one of your organ recitals."

"I remember the voice," he responded with a faint smile. "You spoke to me once about the Island."

"Yes, yours and mine."

Ruth settled him in a chair. His groping hands found the arms and he leaned back resignedly.

"I was looking forward to seeing the Island some day, but now it will never be."

"You can go back there, though, and listen," she said eagerly.

"Do you remember the sounds? The peewits on the moor, the chirping of the oyster catchers on the beach. The waves. I always heard music in them, did you?"

"Yes," he murmured. "Yes, there was music in the waves. Sad, still music, and loud diapasons—"

Ruth Robertson gave Morag a smile of encouragement, as if to say 'Go on'. So she talked more about the island, reviving memories that brought glimmers of response from the listening man.

"Will you come and see me again?" he asked, when she said she must go.

"Yes, I shall. But you must come and see us, too. You know Linnbrae? It's very quiet there and the air is so fresh and pure. Come for tea, you and Miss Robertson."

He shook his head. "Thank you, but I never go anywhere nowadays."

"I could take you there in the car," said his daughter. "It would be an outing for both of us."

He would not give in, however, and the point was not pressed. Morag left well pleased that she had been able to do a little, and hoping the time would come when she could do more.

When she got home Isabel asked where her shopping was.

"I simply hadn't time to shop," she confessed, and over tea she told them about her visit to the organist. They listened with interest, their sympathies aroused.

"What a pity he wouldn't come and see us," remarked Andy.

"There are so many things he could *feel* here, and plenty to listen to."

"Your voice, for one," Brian teased him. "He'd probably get too much of it, as we do."

Just for that, Andy snatched the chocolate biscuit from his plate and crammed it into his mouth. During the scuffle which followed, Isabel jumped up.

"Oh, do pipe down, you two, you'd think this was a zoo!"

She ran from the room and went straight upstairs, to reappear some time later before her mother, who was alone in the sitting room darning socks. Cheeks flushed and eyes bright, the girl looked very bonnie in her red coat and beret.

"I did tell you I was going out, Mummy?"

"Yes, dear." Morag hesitated before asking, "Won't you tell me who you're going to meet?"

Isabel's cheeks flushed pinker. "Well, I suppose you've got every right to ask. It's Hugh Bennett. Any reason why not?"

"Just that he's so much older than you and, well, experienced."

"I don't call that a reason." Her smile was ever so slightly superior. If you mean he's not a silly boy, that's true. He's a very worth-while friend. We understand each other."

Morag felt she had said enough. A friend, yes, but would it stay like that? Her daughter's behaviour recently had pointed to something deeper. It was difficult to know how to handle Isabel; one wrong word might do irreparable damage. Morag sighed and took up her needle again as the door closed behind her daughter.

Strange how the lady of the Manse could not get the thought of Gavin Robertson out of her head. She was still pondering over his sad dilemma when the phone rang on Monday afternoon. It was Ruth Robertson.

"Oh, Mrs. Fleming, I hope you will forgive me for phoning. My father has been talking about you a great deal. He says now that he would love to come and see you in Linnbrae. It's amazing, for up till now he wouldn't stir away from the house. May we come, please?"

Morag said she would be delighted. Her mind worked fast: Tuesday was the flower club, Wednesday the Guild, Thursday a committee meeting, Friday choir practice; but she could fit in their visit in the afternoon—

"Friday, then? We have tea just after five, but come before that—at three if you can manage."

And so it was arranged. Friday turned out to be one of those days in early spring when all nature is awakening to life. You could almost hear the rustle in the garden of things beginning to grow. A chaffinch had been trying out his song all morning to the accompaniment of a great tit's rhythmic challenge. The Linn burn, full and noisy with recent rains, gurgled joyously under the bridge and from the fields came the tremulous baa-ing of newly born lambs.

At three o'clock Miss Robertson's mini-car drew up at the Manse door and Morag went out to greet her visitors.

84

When he alighted, Gavin Robertson stood in the drive with his face upturned to the sun: listening to all the different sounds, while breathing in the fine, crisp air which was so different from the stale atmosphere of town. His hand was on Morag's arm.

"Why does all this remind me of my young days? You are in a lovely place here, nearly as good as our Island."

"I've often thought that," replied his hostess. "Would you care for a walk round? It's really too good to go indoors just yet."

They walked slowly across the glebe. Helped by his stick and Morag's arm he gained more confidence with every step. As he halted on the bridge to listen to the purling of the water, a calmness seemed to descend on him, softening the lines of his face.

"The church is over there," said Morag. "Shall we go in?"

He consented to be led through the churchyard and up the few steps into the building. It had been used for worship for so long, more than two hundred years, that every stick and stone of it was sacred.

"I haven't been in a church since I was ill," he murmured. Then, "What kind of organ have you got here?"

Morag told him, adding, "I'm told it's a good one, but we never hear it at its best. You see, I've got to play it myself and I don't know enough."

She took him over to the keyboard and described the instrument to him.

"Let me hear you play," he said.

She sat down and very tentatively played a verse of 'The Lord's my Shepherd'.

"You see what I mean? I'm afraid to use more than one or two stops."

He was feeling for the organ stool and when she rose he took his place there. Then with seeking fingers he manipulated the stops and began to play the same tune. The same, but how different, for this time it was played by a master hand.

Morag glanced from him to his daughter. She was standing there with trembling lips and tears in her eyes, but they exchanged no words as the blind organist continued to play on. Music like this had never been heard in this little church. As one melody faded on the air another was begun. Some were calm and peaceful but others swelled into triumphant paeans.

Ruth pressed Morag's hand. "It's a miracle," she whispered.

"There's hope for him. Now that he has found music again, he has something to live for."

At last the final notes of 'Praise to the Holiest in the Height' died away and he sat still and silent for long minutes.

They said nothing till he turned to them. "Ruth, are you there?"

"Yes, Father," and she went to him. He put his hand out for hers and Morag heard him say, "Ruth, you have guided me through the shadows, now I am coming into the light again. Bless you, my dear."

As they were moving out of the church the minister came to meet them. He grasped Mr. Robertson's hand.

"I heard some music as I left the manse. It was not my wife's playing. How I wish my whole congregation could have heard it!"

Leaving the visitors with her husband, Morag went to prepare the tea. It was a substantial meal as usual, for the boys always came home ravenous. Seated beside her father,

Ruth saw to his needs. He was not at all helpless, however, and was alert to everything that went on at the table,
actually laughing out once or twice at Andy's remarks.
Ruth was obviously happy at the way he was coming out
of himself, and her pale little face blossomed into un-
suspected beauty.

They took their leave shortly afterwards. Mr. Robertson held on to Morag's hand, saying earnestly:

"Thank you for everything, Mrs. Fleming. Especially
for that time with your organ. It is a treasure. Learn as
much about it as you can."

"I wish I had you to teach me," she confessed.

He patted her hand. "I shall have to start and teach
myself so many things!"

When they had gone, the minister said to his wife:

"I was told our friend had given up his music altogether.
How came it that he was playing in the church?"

"It just happened," she replied. "He heard my crude
attempts and started to show me what the organ could
do. Did you ever hear such wonderful playing?"

"It was an inspiration," he declared.

"To us and to him as well, I think."

Mr. Fleming was not the only one who had heard the
organ that afternoon. Passers-by had halted in the street
to listen. When the choir met that afternoon, they were
all agog.

"We knew it couldn't be you who was playing," they
told Morag, not meaning to be uncomplimentary. "Yon
was a real organist!"

She explained that they had indeed been listening to a
'real' organist and told them who it was.

"Couldn't you ask him to come and give us an organ
recital?" they demanded.

She shook her head. "Mr. Robertson was only playing for himself. He may never play in public again, certainly not in the near future. He is blind and very frail. Will you remember him in your prayers?"

Seeing her earnestness, they promised to do as she asked.

Mrs. Fleming had an arrears of shopping to do next afternoon. This time she took the car and parked it in a Shelton side street. Then she made her way to the big stores, looking guiltily round to see if any Linnbrae people were watching her. It would never do if they reported to Bob Ford, the local grocer, that the lady of the Manse had fallen a prey to the charms of the supermarket. Not that she didn't feel fully justified, for the tinned goods were so much cheaper and one got a better choice. She would never desert Bob for the main groceries, but changes were lightsome.

She was about to enter when she caught sight of Miss Robertson coming towards her, in the company of a good-looking young man. Smiling, she introduced him, "Alan Watson, my fiancé. I am so glad we met you, Mrs. Fleming. I was going to write and tell you about the remarkable change in my father."

"I noticed it myself," said Morag.

"It came so suddenly! Before this, I haven't been able to get out on my own, but today he consented to let the housekeeper stay with him. I never thought I would be free again. I have just been telling Alan that the wedding date might not be so far away after all."

Alan Watson put his hand over hers with a happy smile.

"It can't be too soon for me."

Morag was truly glad for them and happier still to get a

letter shortly afterwards, asking if she would visit the organist again.

"You will find him quite different. He is facing the future with courage now and is finding his way about in a remarkable way. He talks such a lot about you and Linnbrae. In fact, he would like to live there. We have been thinking of a move for some time as this house is far too big and gloomy. Country air suits him, so we may sell up and get somewhere to live near you. Do you mind? Dad will be able to help you with the organ."

"Do I mind?" laughed Morag after reading out the letter to her husband. "I'll welcome them with open arms, won't you? Perhaps some day we'll get that organ recital after all!"

The Talk of the Town

6   Mrs. Fleming was feeling quite gay that
morning. There was no special reason except that the sun
was shining and there were no immediate problems loom-
ing up. The housework was no worry, for Janet Bain was
almost back to normal, having had the plaster removed
from her arm.

"Mind you," she admitted, "I miss it terrible. I was getting quite fond of it. You're looking very chirpy this morning, Mrs. Fleming."

"Am I?" laughed Morag. "Perhaps it's the spring."

"Ach it's just a flash in the pan. The worst of the
winter's to come, take my word for it. It's not good to be
chirpy early in the morning—'Sing before seven, cry before
eleven'."

It was not often that Janet was a prophet of doom.
"Did you get out of bed on the wrong side, Janet?"

"Not me. That man of mine did. He still takes grumpy
turns, though not so bad as he was. However, nobody's
perfect. Will you be going out to the shops? We're need-
ing silver polish."

Having made the beds, Morag set off for the grocer's, still
feeling on top of the world. She really enjoyed shopping in
the village, though with the tempo of life in Linnbrae you
needed time on your hands. Once you got into Bob Ford's
shop, you never knew when you would get out again.

Feeling full of goodwill to everyone, she stepped into

the shop, halting just inside the entrance to examine a stand which Bob kept there with special offers on show. He was selling off some plastic shoppers today in various attractive colours, just what she needed. As she turned them over, choosing a shade to go with her green coat, various remarks from the customers at the counter came to her ears, without making much impact, for she wasn't really listening.

"He's old enough to be her father," said one. "If it was *my* daughter—"

"Wasn't there some kind of scandal long ago?" asked another.

"Aye, his wife—" mumble mumble. "Not as if this was out in the open. A right hole-and-corner business."

"Her mother should put her foot down. It looks bad, being who she is."

"Aye," affirmed the first speaker in a penetrating voice. "I always say that those who live in a Manse should be above reproach."

Morag came to herself with a start, her face flushing crimson. But no one was taking any notice of her: they did not know she was there. There was only one thing to do, leave the shop immediately. She walked into the street, not caring which way she took. Blindly she went on, her feelings in a turmoil.

'If it was *my* daughter.' They must have been referring to Isabel. 'Old enough to be her father.' That of course was Hugh Bennett. So the affair had become common property. These people probably knew more about it than she did herself, or thought they knew. No doubt the whole village was buzzing with gossip, and, of course, those in the Manse would be the last to hear it.

She plunged on, feeling that every eye must be on her.

Up till now, though disturbed about Isabel's friendship with Hugh Bennett, who lived in the nearby town of Shelton, she had supposed that the Linnbrae people were unaware of it. She might have known better.

The Manse affairs were always the subject of gossip; she was used to that, and generally no harm was done. But this was different. Isabel's name was being bandied about and her behaviour censured. She herself was held to blame for letting her daughter go around with a middle-aged man who had a 'scandal' attached to his past. Was she to blame? Could she have done anything to avert it?

Her mind went back to the first time Hugh Bennett had visited the Manse in connection with the broadcast. Isabel had been attracted to him then, she remembered, and he to her. In fact, with the exception of the minister, they had all fallen under his spell. But until he and Isabel turned up that day at the sale of work, Morag had not given the matter another thought. Even when Isabel admitted that they had been seeing each other occasionally, her mother had not been unduly worried. Now, however, things seemed to have taken a serious turn.

Morag did not see what she could have done about it, for the girl had a mind of her own and interference would only have strengthened it. Besides, did she want to interfere? Young ones must have freedom to find out about people for themselves. You could not wrap your children in cotton wool these days.

But perhaps she had been wrong to let things go on outside their ken. If Hugh Bennett was a friend of Isabel's he ought to be a friend of her parents, too. Then nobody would have the right to talk about a 'hole-and-corner' business.

Deciding that the only way to get clear of those prying

eyes, was to forget about the shopping and go home, Morag made her way to the Manse. As she entered the hall the grandfather clock struck eleven and she remembered with a pang how happy she had been a short hour ago. Janet's prognostication had come true.

Her feelings must have shown on her face for when her husband saw her, he immediately asked, "Morag, what's wrong?"

She took him into the sitting room, shedding her coat and shaking out her hair. Then, strangely shaky at the knees, she sat down and told him what she had heard in Bob Ford's shop.

His face showed consternation and disbelief, more so because she had kept Isabel's secret from him, hoping to spare him worry.

"Why didn't you tell me about this before?" he said sternly. "I would have spoken to Isabel."

"She won't be spoken to, Angus. At the moment I think she's bewitched."

His face darkened. "This man has no right to get my daughter talked about. I'll let him know what I think of him."

She had feared this reaction. "You'll antagonise them both if you do that. I don't think there's much wrong with Hugh Bennett. I was rather taken with him myself."

"Oh, you were, were you?" he asked grimly. "Why couldn't the girl take up with someone of her own age? That young divinity student Craig, for instance. He's a fine lad and thinks the world of her."

"Yes, but to her he seems a mere boy. It's Hugh Bennett's age and experience that fascinates her. Also, I think she is sorry for him. Isabel has a very tender heart and the man has had a sad life. He was married, you know, and his wife left him. I don't know the circumstances, but she died later. He must have suffered."

"No doubt," was the reply. "Of course one is sorry for a man in his position, but it's not fair to play on the emotions of a young girl. No, Morag, you must tell her to have nothing more to do with him."

"Then possibly she'll have nothing more to do with us. I'll speak to her certainly, Angus, for I hate the thought of people gossiping."

He nodded gloomily. "The Manse should be 'above reproach', is that what they said? You'd better remind Isabel of that, or would you prefer me to do it?"

Morag said, leave it to her. Angus had given much good advice to the people of his parish but the best of men were liable to make mistakes when it came to their own daughters. Time enough for him to speak to Isabel if she were to fail herself.

But she was not looking forward to the task. Why did girls have to grow up so difficult? Isabel had been such a sweet child, frank and affectionate. In those days her mother had been an all-wise counsellor; now her opinion was seldom asked. And yet the girl must still have regard for her. Hadn't she given her savings towards the purchase of that washing machine? Actions speak louder than words, reflected Morag. Still, there were times when one longed for words as well.

Isabel's present spell of nursing duties kept her from home most of the day. It wasn't worth-while returning for the few hours off in the afternoon, so they were not seeing much of her. It was very late when Morag heard her key in the lock that evening. She had persuaded her husband to go to bed and the boys, of course, had retired long ago. Seeing the light in the sitting room, Isabel came in.

There was something quite breathtaking about her tonight; her eyes and smile were radiant, out of this world. Long ago, Morag had once got a glimpse of herself in the mirror looking exactly like that. She had just fallen in love with the man who was now her husband, and the world was a wonderful place.

"Not in bed yet, Mummy?"

"No, dear." How was she going to begin? "I stayed up to have a talk with you."

Her face closed up. "Oh Mummy, what a bind!"

"Bind or not it's got to be said. Come and sit down, Isabel."

With a bad grace her daughter obeyed. Morag closed the book she had been reading.

"Isabel, the villagers are talking about you and Hugh Bennett. I overheard them in the grocer's this morning."

Crimson mounted Isabel's cheeks and her eyes darted fire.

"Well, what does it matter? Let them talk!"

Morag sighed. "Unfortunately it does matter. With your father being the minister, we ought not to provide food for gossip. One has got to be extra careful."

"That's just the trouble," gloomed the girl. "You can't do a thing, your life's not your own! I've been going to ask if I mightn't take digs in town, go in with some of the other nurses."

Morag had guessed this might be in her mind. "It's not advisable in the meantime, dear. In any case it wouldn't screen you from gossip if—if this friendship goes on."

"Of course it will go on," her daughter declared. "You're

95

not going to ask me to give Hugh up, are you? I'll never do that, never!"

Morag was taken aback by her vehemence. "Does he mean so much to you?" she asked.

"He means everything to me! Yes, it's true. I'm in love with him, Mummy. And he is in love with me. He told me so."

"You're sure—you're sure he meant it?" her mother faltered.

Isabel was very angry. "Of course he meant it! Oh, you just don't understand. You—you and Dad, you live on a different plane."

Morag replied gently, "At least we've got our feet on the ground. And I do understand, Isabel. You're in love and so, you say, is he, but what is it going to lead to?"

"Marriage," was the simple reply. "We'll be getting engaged soon. I wasn't going to tell you yet. It was to stay a lovely secret. A secret's spoiled when you tell people, but since you wanted to know—"

So things had gone even further than Morag feared.

"I hope you have weighed up what such a marriage would mean," she said.

Isabel's head went up proudly. "You don't 'weigh up' things when you're in love."

Her mother might have replied, "That's just what I did do with your father," but it would have been useless. She deliberated before replying:

"Well, engagement or not, you can't go on meeting Hugh Bennett in Shelton without bringing him here, so that we can get to know him properly. Invite him to the Manse, Isabel. It's got to come out in the open, or they'll just go on talking."

Her daughter was very unwilling. The 'open' would

dissolve some of the magic.

"Hugh doesn't like Linnbrae. It's that sister-in-law of his. He says she's a menace."

Morag's lips twitched. She had no reason to like the lady in question either.

"Exactly my sentiments. But he does not need to meet her."

"I'll see what he says," promised Isabel.

Hugh Bennett came to the Manse to meet the family on the following Saturday, as it was Isabel's free week-end. The fire in the big lounge which they seldom used, was lit for the occasion.

Morag could see that Isabel was very strung up, but Hugh Bennett's manner revealed nothing but its customary ease and courtesy.

One could not help being attracted by this man with the handsome, careworn face and expressive dark eyes. Morag was drawn to him once more, but the minister's greeting was restrained, as one might expect. After some conversation he begged to be excused and went upstairs to his study. Hugh Bennett turned to Morag, asking frankly:

"I hope Mr. Fleming hasn't gone because of me?"

"Not at all," replied Morag. "He'll have some revision to do to his sermon for tomorrow. He's a perfectionist, you know."

"Yes, I would guess that. It's a virtue I'm afraid I don't possess, though I admire it in others." He gave her one of his warm, sudden smiles. "Mrs. Fleming, I'm afraid you're a bit worried about me and Isabel. What is it that bothers you?"

It was difficult to explain. "Well, the difference in your

ages, mostly." He pressed the hand of the girl by his side.

"Yes, there is a big gap. But Isabel doesn't mind that; do you, darling?"

Looking at him with her heart in her eyes she replied:

"I'm glad of it, Hugh."

"You see," he went on, "Isabel is mature for her years and I have felt much younger since I met her, so perhaps the gap is not so wide. But be frank with me, Mrs. Fleming, have you heard things about the past that put you off?"

She admitted it was true.

"I was unhappily married," he confessed. "We were misfits and brought out the worst in each other. It does happen, you know. When my wife left me there was a flood of gossip, but none of it was true. I've explained this to Isabel, and she believes me. I hope you do, too."

His voice was so earnest and appealing that she could not doubt him. "Of course I believe you."

"Then," he said, with his arm round Isabel, "you and Mr. Fleming have no objection to our engagement?"

Still with a niggling doubt, "Would it make any difference if we had?"

"Would it, dear?" he asked Isabel.

"Not a bit of difference," she declared.

Morag said slowly, "Well, it seems there's no help. I'll speak to the minister."

"Would you like me to do it?" Hugh asked.

"Later you can have a talk with him. I'll break the ice." She got up. "Would you two like to go for a walk while I get the tea ready?"

They seemed glad to escape, going down the drive arm in arm, Isabel's glowing face upturned to his. They were in love all right, no doubt about that.

Morag went into the kitchen to start her preparations.

While she was putting on the kettle, her husband appeared.

"They've gone out," she told him. "Angus, it's no use our holding out against them. We'll have to agree to this engagement or we'll lose Isabel."

"It looks as if we'd lost her already," he replied sadly. "Very well, Morag, if you think it wise, I'll raise no objection to an engagement. But no marriage as yet. The two are not congenial, whatever you may say. I can only hope that Isabel will find that out before it's too late."

The meal was ready and they were waiting for the pair to return when the doorbell rang.

"It can't be them. Isabel has her key," said Morag going to the door.

A young man stood on the step, slight in build, with fair hair bunched on his brow and shy blue eyes. Peter Craig smiled at her, asking eagerly:

"Mrs. Fleming, is Isabel at home?"

She had to tell him that her daughter was out, though she did not stay with whom. His face fell.

"Oh, dear. Will she be long, do you think?"

"Probably not." To ask him in would make things awkward.

"Perhaps I'll see her tomorrow, then. I'm in Linnbrae for the week-end."

"Yes, she'll be at home tomorrow, but—"

She stopped in confusion, for Isabel and Hugh Bennett were coming up the drive, their arms linked lovingly.

The young man saw them, too. A painful flush suffused his face and he looked round as if for flight.

"I'd better go," he stammered.

Morag felt heart sorry for him. "Wait and be introduced, Peter," she said, laying a comforting hand on his arm.

The two came up looking in the seventh heaven. Isabel smiled at Peter.

"Hello, Peter. Have you and Dad been having a session?" The young man occasionally came to the minister for advice about his studies. Still embarrassed, he replied:

"Not really. I'm just going—"

Hugh Bennett smiled at him paternally, as Morag introduced the two, then he was off like a shot towards the gate.

"Is anything wrong with Peter?" Isabel asked, too caught up in her own happiness to realise what she had done to him.

"I think he may have been studying too hard," Morag said non-committally.

The notice of the engagement appeared in the *Shelton Advertiser*, but Linnbrae's special grapevine spread the news long before that. Morag was conscious of a certain restraint in the good wishes which came their way. Peter Craig's Aunt Jean was sympathetic. She was always frank with Morag, her best friend.

"I wish it were Peter. Do you think Isabel will be happy with Hugh Bennett, Morag?"

"She's happy just now and so is he. It might work out all right."

"Poor dear, you're worried, aren't you? I've always envied you your family—" she had no children of her own—"but when it comes to a time like this I can see what I'm spared. But cheer up, as long as they don't want to get married right away, she has time to change her mind!"

The conversation took place at the Guild meeting. Sylvia Bennett was also present and she approached Morag with a smile which was slightly forced.

"Well, I hear your daughter has brought it off," she observed. "Very bright of her to land my brother-in-law. He's considered quite a catch, you know. Still, he's so much older, I'm surprised you gave your consent. Does her grandmother know?"

"Not yet," Morag informed her stiffly. She was not looking forward to informing Angus's mother of the engagement. When she wrote the customary fortnightly letter she was careful to say nothing about it. Perhaps it was cowardice, but she preferred to get used to the idea herself before coping with the old lady's objections, for objections there were bound to be.

However, she had not counted on Sylvia Bennett. One forenoon when she and Janet were busy spring-cleaning the dining room, the telephone rang. She waited, thinking Angus might answer it, but he did not oblige, so she got down off the steps and went herself. At first she could not believe it was his mother on the line from Dumfries, for she seldom used the phone for long distance.

"This is serious news, Morag! Is it actually true?"

Well she knew what the rebuking voice referred to.

"Perfectly true, though I can't think how you got to know."

"Sylvia Bennett wrote me. It ought to have come from you, of course. Have you and Angus gone out of your minds?"

"Gran," she replied, "Angus and I could not help it."

"Nonsense, you ought to have laid down the law. I am coming to see you tomorrow. *I'll* have a talk with Isabel. She'll listen to me."

"No, Gran, she won't. Please don't come!"

Her plea was useless. Old Mrs. Fleming gave the time of her train's arrival and asked to be met at Shelton. Right in the middle of the spring-cleaning! But more than the cleaning would be disrupted, she knew.

She met her next day with the car. During the journey to Linnbrae the interrogation about Hugh Bennett went on. Isabel was the favourite grandchild; she had always taken her grandmother's admonitions with a good grace and responded to the rare touches of affection from the stern old lady.

"He sounds the last sort of man the child should marry. She must not be allowed to throw away her life like this, don't you see that?"

"It's not my will," sighed Morag. "Isabel is very determined. She is deeply in love. To say too much against Hugh Bennett would hurt her intolerably. Besides, there is very little against him. He is a very charming man."

"Charm!" echoed the other. "A fatal gift, Morag. It does more harm than many a vice."

Morag had not informed Isabel of the reason for her grandmother's visit, though no doubt she guessed it. The old lady stayed up late to have it out with her when she came home.

"Mother," appealed her son, "things have gone too far now for you to argue with Isabel. I would much rather you didn't."

The plea was useless. "If you and Morag had done your duty in the first place, there would be no need for me to speak at all," she said.

"Gran," Morag put in, "our children don't ask us whom they should marry. Angus didn't ask you if he could marry me, did he?"

For a moment the old lady was taken aback. Then, "No ... if he had—"

She halted there, but Morag knew she was going to say,

"I would have put a stop to it."

She had never approved of her daughter-in-law. Occasionally she had seemed to soften, but never for long. With encouragement Morag would have met her half-way —more than half-way—and it was still her hope that a real understanding would come about some day.

It was not to be on this visit, however.

Isabel came in, tired with her long day's nursing and in no mood to face renewed opposition. Her grandmother insisted on speaking to her alone and Morag and Angus left them together in the sitting room. Exactly what took place in there they were never to know, but fifteen minutes later the door was thrown open and their daughter burst out, her cheeks flaming. She stamped into the kitchen where her parents were waiting.

"I can't stand it any longer! You two asked Gran to come here, didn't you? You thought she might persuade me to give Hugh up when you had failed?"

Morag said placatingly, "Isabel, you are quite wrong. We didn't even tell Gran you were engaged. Somebody else did." And that somebody, she thought, had a lot to answer for. "Believe me, we were against Gran saying anything to you at all."

But her words did nothing to mollify the angry girl.

"I'll never forgive her for saying such things, never! The sooner Hugh and I get married the better." And she ran out of the kitchen and up to her room.

Angus stopped Morag from going after her. "Let her cool down," he advised. "We'll probably have to cool Mother down too." He heaved a sigh. "Morag, what has happened to the little girl we knew?"

"That's what I've just been asking myself. We go on for years thinking nothing will ever change. But that's only a delusion; things keep changing all the time."

She took up the kettle to fill it at the sink, for a cup of tea was a great help in any crisis. But Angus took the kettle out of her hand and laid it on the stove. Then he put his arms round her and drew her close.

"*You* do not change, Morag. Our love does not change. Thank God for that," and he gave her a kiss full of comfort and reassurance.

A Bunch of Daffodils

7   IT WAS THE AFTERNOON OF THE 'DAFFODIL Teas', the annual spring sale held by the Woman's Guild before they disbanded for the summer. As usual, Morag Fleming was in the thick of the fray. No matter how troubled she might be about family problems, the work of the church must go on.

She and Mrs. Conway were in charge of the flower stall, which included masses of daffodils donated from the gardens of Linnbrae. Daffodils were Morag's favourite flower. They came at a time when people needed cheering up. Their colour suggested sunshine and all the gay things of life. And how bravely they tossed their heads when storms tried to beat them down! No wonder the poet Wordsworth was inspired by them to write his famous poem—'I wandered lonely as a cloud—'

It was about the only poem Morag remembered from her school days. She had never been studious and her education had stopped at an early age. She had learned a great deal since, of course, from life if not from books. But she often felt very ignorant compared with her husband and her son Brian, who was about to sit for his 'Highers' very soon.

Occasionally, Morag had tried to 'improve' herself but every attempt to amass knowledge was doomed to failure. There was so much else to do, so many demands on her time.

So there she was, knowing only one poem. But she did

know it by heart and it brought her great comfort at times, just as it had the poet. She had only to close her eyes and imagine bright visions of golden daffodils, 'fluttering and dancing in the breeze' and she at once felt calm and hopeful.

No need to conjure up visions today, however, for the daffodils were here beside her, stacked in basins and pails, getting a quick sale. There was a big crowd in the hall and it looked as if they might make quite a lot of money for the fabric fund.

Repairs in the vestibule and the vestry, where the dry rot had been found, were now in hand, but the thermometer on the graph which showed the sum required, had still a long way to climb.

Before they were quite sold out, Morag chose some fine, large blooms and put them in a corner behind the stall. Not for herself. There were still some of the short, half-wild variety among the grass in the glebe which would do for the Manse. These were for a special member of the congregation who had been in her thoughts for a long time.

There, the bulk of the flowers were gone now, only a few broken blossoms, scattered leaves and bare stems were left on the stall which was well splashed with water. The tea-tables were stripped of food, the cakes and candy had also disappeared. Tired but happy, the stall-holders had started to count over the takings.

"Any daffodils left, Mrs. Fleming?"

The speaker was a precise looking lady in a neat grey costume and felt hat. A person of standing in Linnbrae, Miss Ellen Simpson was a retired headmistress known for her intellectual abilities and her prowess as a public speaker. Morag admired her greatly and often wished she had some of her cleverness and assurance.

"I'm sorry, Miss Simpson," she replied, "you are just too late. I would have kept some daffodils for you if you had warned me."

But the lady had spied the flowers in the corner.

"You've got some over there, haven't you?"

"Yes, but I'm reserving these."

Miss Simpson's eyebrows contracted. She was accustomed to getting what she wanted.

"But they're just what I need! You may put an extra shilling on the cost, if you like."

Perhaps it was bad business, but there was something in her manner which made Morag stick to her point.

"I really can't give you them, Miss Simpson. If only you'd come sooner!"

"You seemed to have plenty last time I looked. Oh well, I suppose it can't be helped."

But it was said in a punishing kind of way which made Morag feel about ten years old.

"Miss Simpson makes me quail," remarked Mrs. Conway as the lady moved off. "I'm glad I was never a pupil of hers. May I ask who the daffodils are for?"

"I heard that Mrs. Maxwell was ill. Perhaps you don't know her? She lives at Greenside."

"I haven't met her yet. She keeps herself to herself, doesn't she? I've heard plenty about her, though."

Morag smiled. "And not to her advantage, I expect. She's a person one can't get through to at all. I've been trying hard ever since we came here."

Mrs. Maxwell was one of Morag's few failures. She was a bit of a mystery woman who had alienated all her neighbours. When she did emerge from her retreat it was only to find fault. She had refused every offer of friendship and for a long time had not attended church. Nowadays people had stopped bothering about her. Let her sink or swim; she had made her bed and she could lie on it!

"That's all very well," Morag had confided to her husband, "but she looks such a thoroughly unhappy woman. I'm sure she could be helped if one knew the way."

"If anyone can find a way, it will be you," the minister replied. "All my efforts have been in vain."

Morag was glad he had such faith in her, but after several attempts to break the ice, she had almost given up. Almost, not quite, for when she had heard of Mrs. Maxwell's illness, she decided to have another try.

The news had not come direct to the Manse. People who took ill seemed to think that the minister should know it by instinct. Then, if he didn't visit, it was a black mark against him. To avoid this, Morag always kept her eyes and ears open. She came by most of the village news in the grocer's shop. Some of it was quite shattering, as on the day she'd overheard them discussing her daughter's friendship with Hugh Bennett.

Now that Isabel and Hugh were engaged and her girl was wearing a handsome solitaire diamond ring, the gossip had died down, which was a blessing. After her indignation at her grandmother's unwanted advice, Isabel had apologised to her parents and to her grandmother too, though that lady was assured that nothing would ever make her change her mind. Old Mrs. Fleming had departed from the Manse in high dudgeon and relations were very strained indeed. But at the moment Isabel was all sweetness and light: there was always that to be thankful for.

Mrs. Maxwell's illness, it appeared, had not been known

till one day when she took in her milk at teatime, clad in a dressing gown. Next day, Dr. Campbell's car was at the door. That was all they had to go by, for when her next door neighbour had knocked at the door, she got no reply.

Greenside was a row of old-fashioned cottages near the church. Some of them had bits of garden, but Mrs. Maxwell's at the end had nothing but grass. She must sometimes yearn for a flower, thought Morag as she left the hall carrying that last bunch of daffodils. When she reached the cottage it was to find the curtains drawn and everything silent. Usually the folk here left their doors open on a good day, but Mrs. Maxwell's was shut tight. The brass bell and letter box were tarnished and everything had a neglected air.

Without much hope, Morag rang the bell three times. No response, so she made her way round to the backdoor. It was the same here, silence and neglect. There was no bell, so she knocked repeatedly, with no result. Looking in her handbag for a scrap of paper she found a receipted bill and wrote on the back:

"Sorry you are ill. Please accept these daffodils. Best wishes from Morag Fleming."

Then she put the daffodils on the kitchen window-sill with the note attached. As she was leaving, a tiny opening appeared between the curtains and for a split second she saw a face. Then it was gone. So Mrs. Maxwell wasn't dead or even bed-bound. She was just being difficult as usual. No wonder her neighbours had given her up!

Morag went home, wondering if the unhappy woman would even condescend to take the daffodils into her house. Perhaps they would have been better with Miss Simpson after all!

* * *

A few nights later, the minister came home from a meeting of the 'Men's Own' with a proposition which took Morag's breath away.

"The men are arranging to have a Brains Trust night to end the season," he said. "We'll sell tickets for it and the money will go to the fabric fund. They don't want the Woman's Guild to get all the glory!"

"A very good idea," agreed his wife. "If they get good speakers on the panel, it should go well."

"Yes, indeed. They're going to ask Thomson, the burgh councillor, and Dr. Campbell, both eloquent speakers. Then they hope to get someone connected with broad-casting. They suggested Hugh Bennett, Isabel."

His daughter looked up with a bright smile. "I'll ask him, if you like, Dad. If he can't come himself, he might know someone who can."

"That's fine, Isabel. They need a fourth speaker and as there will be a mixed audience, they've decided to invite a woman."

"Wonderful," laughed his wife. The Men's Own was very much not-at-home to women as a rule. "I suppose they'll be asking Miss Simpson. She's the only brainy woman hereabouts."

Her husband sat down and took off his shoes before answering.

"Miss Simpson's name was suggested, but it wasn't well received. As a matter of fact," his grey eyes twinkled at her, "they are very keen to have the lady of the Manse."

Morag threw back her head. "Me, on a Brains Trust! You're joking!"

Andy also thought it very funny. He was curled up in an armchair making himself invisible, for it was long past his bedtime. His giggle gave him away.

"At least you'd give them entertainment, Mum!"

The minister eyed him. "Make yourself scarce, young man. And let me tell you that your mother has a lot more in that small head than you give her credit for."

"Yes, Dad." He went slowly out of the room, grinning back at them. "You'll be saying *I've* got brains next!"

"I only wish you'd give us reason to say it," his father riposted. "It's true, Morag, the men wouldn't consider anyone but you. A great compliment, if you ask me."

"Yes, Mummy," agreed Isabel. "You've got a lot of staunch admirers. It's a wonder Dad's not jealous."

"What blethers." Morag was blushing like a girl. "I can't possibly do it, Angus. I'd disgrace myself and you, for life."

"They'll be very disappointed," he told her. "I was asked to use all my persuasive powers on you. As for brains, I wouldn't worry. There will be lots of questions you can answer. Shall I tell them you'll agree?"

"You've got to," declared her daughter. "Don't you see, it's a challenge."

Morag's life seemed to be full of challenges; she was always having to rise to them. It would have been nice to sit back for a while, now that the winter's work was coming to an end. She started to make excuses. She was tired after the Daffodil Teas and the spring-cleaning. The Guild outing had to be put in hand.

"Oh, and hundreds of other things, Angus. I simply haven't the time!"

"But this doesn't need time, only two hours on the night," he pleaded. "I'll be chairing the meeting myself. I'll make it easy for you."

She had always found it difficult to say no to him. Perhaps it was her duty. The men wouldn't think much of her if she turned them down. As Angus said, they were paying her a compliment, an unheard of honour.

"Oh, very well," she gave in at last. "But if I'm a flop, as I'm sure to be, you can tell them they asked for it!"

During the next week or two Morag was to regret her decision over and over again. Every morning it was the first thing that popped into her head. "You've to sit on that platform with all those people gaping at you, waiting for you to make a fool of yourself. It'll be worse than the broadcast. You'll never get through it, never! What on earth possessed you?"

The thought would recur at intervals during the day and the butterflies inside her would start up again. Her last waking wish at night was that she might catch flu or sprain her ankle and thus have an honourable excuse for calling off. As the big night approached she got more and more desperate. Then, as if she did not feel bad enough, one day she ran into Miss Simpson in the village. She would have slipped past with a short greeting, but the lady stopped short, confronting her.

"I understand that you are to be on the panel tomorrow night," she remarked.

Morag had heard that Miss Simpson was very annoyed that she had not been invited to take part herself and the tone of her voice bore that out.

"Yes, that's so," replied Morag. "I can't think why."

"As the minister's wife you possibly have priority. I don't envy you, you know."

"Really! Why don't you?"

"It's a most nerve-racking ordeal. I have sat on many panels myself and I know. Have you had any experience?"

"Well, not exactly," Morag confessed.

"Pity. Experience helps, you know. You've got to have a good background of knowledge, too. I suppose you've got that?"

Morag smiled bravely. "My knowledge is rather chaotic, I'm afraid."

"Oh, dear. It's invaluable to have a clear brain on such occasions. All your information filed and docketed, ready at a moment's notice. I've got a very orderly brain myself."

"I'm sure you have," observed the lady of the Manse. "Mine is like a ragbag, but I'll get through, I suppose!"

She wasn't going to admit to the butterflies, not under the pitying gaze of Miss Simpson.

"Also," went on the unrelenting voice, "you've got to be a quick thinker and able to express yourself. Otherwise, you won't get a word in edgeways."

"You make it sound very alarming," Morag put in.

"Well, I thought I should warn you," declared the other. "But don't let what I've said put you off. I'll be there to see how you acquit yourself. I'm looking forward to it."

Morag was sure she was. If anything more was needed to put her in a panic, it was that encounter.

After tea, as a last resort, she went up to Brian's room where he was studying, and asked him for a loan of his Encyclopedia. She brought it down and sat with it on her knee, gathering up pieces of knowledge at random, from A to Z.

"Do you think there might be a question about Anthropology?" she asked her husband who was preoccupied with a book.

"I wouldn't think so."

"Oh, good." She went on to the Hs. "The Hottentots, perhaps?"

"Definitely not."

She had a look through the Rs. "Rats, then?"

"Rats?" Angus came to life. "Morag, what's that you're reading?"

"Just the Encyclopedia," she confessed.

He burst out laughing. "Put it away, dear, it will only confuse you."

"But I've got to know *something*! Miss Simpson says—"

"So you have been listening to her, have you? Forget what she says; you know more than she does. Go to bed early and have a good night's sleep. It will do you far more good than an Encyclopedia."

Morag sighed but obeyed.

It was with a feeling of desperation that she dressed herself for the ordeal next evening. Last spring's green suit with a chic little hat to match gave her a momentary lift and when Angus said she didn't look a minute older than the day they had first met, the glow of the compliment kept her going till she was installed on the hall platform along with the rest of the panel. Then as she realised that the moment was upon her, the glow suddenly departed, leaving her cold and shivery.

The hall was crowded. There before her were the rows of faces she had pictured. Eager, waiting faces, some friendly, others not so friendly. She felt very much alone perched up here, in spite of her three companions: Dr. Campbell with a large grin on his face, the councillor who had a pompous, important air, and a friend of Hugh Bennett, who had not been able to come himself. His name was Bryden Foster and he looked very knowledgable. In fact, they didn't need her at all. Would they miss her very much if she slipped out of the side door and disappeared?

Oh, dear, there was Miss Simpson right in front, her eagle eye upon her. Morag gripped her hands together tensely. It was eight o'clock. Before ten it would be over—if she could last out that long!

The minister was speaking now, introducing the members of the panel, including herself. Then the audience were asked to put their questions. They had them written on slips of paper and came up to the front one by one and read them out.

The first was a query about the common market, to which the councillor gave a brilliant reply with the two men chipping in. When asked what her opinion was, Morag frankly confessed that she didn't know a thing about it. The audience seemed amused and Miss Simpson smiled a very superior smile.

As the questions proceeded, Morag occasionally managed to blurt out something, but after a sentence or two she completely dried up, whereas these others could go on for hours, it seemed. The councillor waxed eloquent about housing, Mr. Foster about television, and the doctor about dangerous drugs; but the lady of the Manse just sat there wishing the ground would open and swallow her up.

When she saw Miss Simpson step forward to put her question, Morag felt her last moment had come.

"Will each member of the panel tell us what is their favourite poem and quote from it?"

A stab of hope went through her. Perhaps Miss Simpson had meant to catch her out, but she hadn't! She did have a favourite poem and she could quote from it, too. In fact she'd give them the whole of it. That would show them!

As usual, Bryden Foster got in first, with a sonnet from

Shakespeare. Then Dr. Campbell gave them a bit from Tennyson and the councillor quoted from Browning about 'Grow old along with me, the best is yet to be—'

"And Mrs. Fleming," encouraged her husband, "I think you have a favourite poem?"

Morag nodded. "Yes, I have." She swallowed nervously. "It's Wordsworth's 'Daffodils'." And she began, "I wandered lonely as a cloud." She stopped there. Nothing more would come. Every single word of the poem she knew so well had vanished into thin air. She began again.

"I wandered lonely as a cloud—" But it was hopeless.

"That floats on high," prompted the minister in a stage whisper.

"That floats on high," repeated Morag, her mouth dry. "I'm sorry, but I've forgotten the rest."

Everybody laughed. Miss Simpson looked triumphant. The last word was with her, after all.

"I'm a failure," Morag announced, back in the Manse. "I should never have been talked round to do it. I'll never live it down."

The minister replied kindly, "Oh, come, Morag, you did splendidly. You raised a few laughs, what more could you want?"

"You're right, I made myself a laughing stock. I'll be afraid to face anyone in the street after this. Tell the men they ought to have asked Miss Simpson."

Her husband patted her hand. "You're taking it far too seriously. After all, it was only an entertainment."

"For you, perhaps. It was anything but entertainment for me."

Next day she still felt disgraced and decided to stay indoors. It would be terrible if she were to go out and meet Miss Simpson. She would relax with Woman's Hour and her knitting and try to forget.

But towards three o'clock the doorbell rang. Angus was out and she would have to go. Switching off the wireless she went reluctantly through the hall and opened the door. She could hardly believe her eyes when she saw who was there.

"Mrs. Maxwell! I'm delighted to see you. Please do come in."

The thin, brittle woman with the tight lips and haggard face, hesitated :

"Mrs. Fleming, could I speak to you alone?"

"Of course. There's no one in but me. Come into the sitting room, it's cosy there."

The visitor sat down on the edge of the chair at the fire, clutching her handbag. It was obvious she was in a highly nervous state.

"I haven't been out of my house for weeks, till last night," she began.

"Last night? You were in the hall? I didn't see you."

"I was in a corner at the back."

"I was so nervous I only saw the people in front," explained Morag with a laugh. "I oughtn't to have been there at all. I let the team down, I'm afraid."

The other leaned forward. "I'm glad you were there. That was why I went, to see and hear you. You brought me daffodils when I was feeling low. Very low, Mrs. Fleming, not only in body but in mind."

Morag said, "I'm so sorry. But I'm glad you got the daffodils all right."

"You were gone when I opened the door. I don't usually open the door at all."

"But you ought to, Mrs. Maxwell, Folks want to be friendly."

"No, I've made myself hated. I'm nasty to people, I can't help myself. Mrs. Fleming, last night I felt you were the kind of person I could confide in. You were so different. You weren't trying to be clever."

Morag chuckled. "Believe me, even if I did try, I could never be clever."

Her visitor gave a little smile. "The doctor advised me to get out of my shell, Mrs. Fleming, and I don't know how to set about it. Will you help me?"

"Certainly, if I can. Perhaps if you could tell me how it all began—"

The story came out haltingly. It had to do with the death of her husband and the behaviour of his family, a sad tale of jealousy and pride on both sides.

"I can't bear it any longer," she sighed. "What do you think I should do?"

"Couldn't you make peace with your husband's people?" Morag suggested. "Then your mind would be at rest. You'd feel better in every way."

Mrs. Maxwell sat silently struggling with herself. Then, in a toneless whisper she said, "It would be very difficult."

"Try, anyway. But whatever you do, Mrs. Maxwell, please feel that you can come to me or my husband any time."

Hesitantly, the visitor replied, "But your husband is such a good man, perhaps he wouldn't understand the—the terrible thoughts I sometimes have."

"He would, I'm sure he would," said Morag earnestly.

There were more confidences and a friendly cup of tea before Mrs. Maxwell took her leave, already much comforted. She would be at church on Sunday, she said.

"And thank you again for the daffodils, and everything."

Morag waved to her from the door, then went back to her knitting in quite a different frame of mind. Amazingly, last night's sense of failure had fled. It did not seem to matter any more that she had not shone in the Brains Trust. Neither did Miss Simpson's opinion count for anything. What did matter was that she had at last got through to the woman who had sealed herself off for so long from friendship and love.

A Debt of Gratitude

8 THE FAMILY HAVING DEPARTED, THE MINISTER
and his wife were alone at the table that June morning
when the post arrived. There was a letter for each of
them. Mrs. Fleming read hers with satisfaction. It was
confirmation of the booking they had made for their
August holiday in the island of Arran.

When the family were small, they had always rented a
house for themselves, but now that the boys were old
enough to obey the rules, Morag found a boarding house
more restful. For the lady of the Manse, the old sort of
holiday had merely been 'a change of sink'.

"Good, Angus! Cairndhu can have us again. It was
touch and go; we nearly left it too late. Are you listening?"

"Yes, of course, dear." But he was deep in his own
letter.

"This is from my successor in the Briarsford Church.
Remember him?"

Of course she remembered the man who had taken her
husband's place, and the busy town of Briarsford, too.
They had gone straight there after their marriage and
the youthful bride had shed many a tear over the strange-
ness of it all.

The minister went on, "He tells me that two of our old
parishioners are coming to Linnbrae to live: Mr. and Mrs.
Purdie."

"Oh, Angus, that's wonderful! I've often wondered how

they were getting on. They were marvellously kind to me."

Just how kind they had been, even Angus could not know, for she had never confessed to him the utter loneliness that had assailed her, going straight from her peaceful native island to the dust and bustle of the workaday town where she knew nobody and nobody knew her. Her position as minister's wife was quite new to her and she made mistakes which were criticised unfairly by certain people in the church.

On one of her worst days, Morag had been walking along the street with tears in her eyes, when a cheerful voice greeted her. She had stopped and smiled shakily.

"You'll not know who I am." The woman who spoke had the kindest face she had ever seen. "We sit in the middle pews of the church, near the front. Purdie's the name."

The tone was motherly, the smile like soothing balm to her troubled spirit.

"Yes, of course, Mrs. Purdie. I remember you now."

The other, with a hand on her wrist, drew her out of the crowd.

"Poor wee lassie, you're gey young to have so much thrust upon you all at once. Look, I live up here above the shops: what about coming in for a cup of tea?"

That cup of tea had been the saving of her. Mrs. Purdie seemed to know instinctively what she was going through and gave her a lot of sane advice as well as sympathy. Later, Morag got to to know her husband too and he was just the same. Quietly and doucely the pair of them sat in their pew Sunday after Sunday, their listening faces upturned to the pulpit, intent on every word that came from the minister's lips. They had a son and a daughter in their early teens, Morag recalled.

"I don't think I ever came across such genuinely 'good' people as the Purdies," she told her husband now. "They had only one desire in the world, remember? Both of them had a terrific urge to go abroad some day, just once."

"I wonder if they ever managed it," mused her husband.

"They were saving up for it and intended to go when the children were off their hands. Oh, I do hope they got their wish."

"You'll find out before long," said Angus Fleming, and he was right, for a Sunday or two later Morag caught sight of her old friends in the congregation, when she sat back from the organ to give her attention to the sermon.

There, near the back of the church, sat the woman to whom she would always owe a debt of gratitude. Over seventy now, her hair snow-white, Mrs. Purdie still had the same serenity on her ageing face, the same promise of comfort in her smiling glance. Morag's heart went out to her as it had done long ago and the minute the service was over she went down the aisle to greet her.

"I can't tell you how happy we are to have you with us, Mrs. Purdie. It's been a long time since the day you gave me that cup of tea."

"Ay, so it has. But you're not much older looking for all that, Mrs. Fleming."

"Thank you! I'm a lot wiser, I hope," laughed the other. "How is your husband? He's not with you."

"No, Willie's not so well. That's why we left Briarsford. The doctor thought he'd be better with country air."

"He'll flourish here all right. We've simply got to have a good gabble, Mrs. Purdie. Can you come to the Manse tomorrow afternoon? Your husband, too, if he's able."

Her face glowed. "The wee walk will do him good.

Thanks, Mrs. Fleming, it's nice to think you haven't forgotten us."

As if she ever could, thought Morag next day as she looked out her best china and the silver teapot. Nothing was too good for her expected visitors. When she saw them coming up the drive she went down to take Mr. Purdie's arm. Though he looked ill and worn he still had his old chuckle, and they were soon chatting easily over the teacups.

"Tell me all about yourselves and the family," bade Morag. "I remember you had one big wish, long ago—to go abroad. Did you ever manage it?"

A small, rueful smile passed between husband and wife. Mrs. Purdie shook her head.

"We've had to give up that dream," she said. "Once Jenny and Calum were married we got ready for our big fling, but my mother became ill and we took her in. When she passed over and we were alone again, we might have managed it, but a sad thing happened. Calum's wife died —a lovely girl she was. It was a terrible shock and he was left with the wee girlie, Judy."

"Our grand-daughter," put in her husband with a fond, proud note in his voice. "She stayed with us while Calum was overseas on business. Three years—or was it four, Annie?"

"Three and a half," was the reply, "till Calum married again. It was better for the lass to have a real home, but we missed her sore. She was the light of our lives. Show Mrs. Fleming her picture, Willie."

From a worn pocket book Mr. Purdie took a colour snapshot of a small girl with bright eyes and brown curls.

"That's her, Mrs. Fleming—isn't she bonnie? And such an old-fashioned wee case! Never called us Granny and

Grandpa like other kids. It was always 'Grandmamma and Grandpapa'. Smart too, top of the class every time. She's older now, of course. What age would she be, Annie?"

"Sixteen last April," was the prompt reply, "quite the young lady. We don't see much of her now," for a moment her voice faltered, "but it won't be long till we do. Funny you should ask us about going abroad, Mrs. Fleming."

"You mean, you're still hoping?"

She laughed. "Oh no, we're reconciled to the fact that it will never be, not for us. Willie couldn't stand up to it now. But wee Judy got the chance to go on a cruise with the school and was going to be so disappointed if she didn't get, so we are putting up the money."

To see their faces, you would think they were getting money instead of giving it. With this gesture they were probably throwing away their last chance of fulfilling a lifetime wish, but there was no sign of regret, just thankfulness that they were able to do it.

"Then," went on Mrs. Purdie, "when Judy comes back from the cruise, she's coming to stay with us for a wee while before she returns to school, and we'll hear all about it. We're looking forward to that, I can tell you!"

"I'm sure you are." Morag poured out fresh tea and urged them to have another piece of her jam sponge. "All I can say is that Judy is a fortunate girl to have such nice grandparents."

During the summer weeks before they went to Arran, Mrs. Fleming saw a lot of the Purdies and grew very fond of them. On a fine day Mr. Purdie sat on a chair outside the cottage drinking in the sights and sounds of the countryside. Though he would never be really strong, you could see the change was doing him good and Annie was grateful. She had a knack of seeing to all his needs without fussing over him and still gave him little jobs to do to keep him from feeling too helpless.

A wise woman, one who had loved and served all her life with no thought of return, the salt of the earth, thought Morag.

Every time they met, the talk veered round to their adored grand-daughter, Judy. They counted the days till she would be leaving on the cruise and they had the atlas constantly on hand picking out the ports she would call at on the Mediterranean, places that had fascinated them both for countless years and which they would never see. But Judy would see them. Judy would come back and tell them all her adventures.

Morag was very busy getting ready to go off on their own holiday. A retired minister from Shelton would be taking Angus's pulpit for three or four Sundays. Mr. Robertson, the blind organist, and his daughter Ruth, were now occupying the bungalow they had bought in Linnbrae and he had promised to take over the organ for the time being. It was a great relief to Morag, her only regret being that she would be unable to hear him play herself, but she hoped to do so later on.

She was disappointed that Isabel would not be coming with them to Arran. Her holidays were scheduled for a later date and no doubt she would be going somewhere with her fiancé. It was the first break in the family holiday, but, like all mothers, she could not expect to keep her fledglings permanently in the nest.

Brian was certainly going to enjoy his holiday this year. Word had just come that he had passed his Highers and would be going to the university in October. Between his exams and the time of the results, he had been going around with a face of doom, but now they could depart with easy minds.

In spite of the scores of odds and ends to be seen to, Morag took time off on the day before their departure to say goodbye to the Purdies. The cottage door was open, so she tapped and called, "Anybody in?"

"Come right ben," came Mrs. Purdie's voice.

Willie was sitting inside today. For once his smile did not come spontaneously. Looking round, Morag caught sight of a gaily coloured postcard on the mantelpiece showing a Mediterranean scene.

"So you've heard from Judy. How is she enjoying herself?"

"Fine. She's having a grand time." The brightness in Annie's voice seemed slightly forced. "Good of her to send us a postcard, wasn't it? You know how young girls hate to write."

Still, thought Morag, a letter would have been better, more grateful.

"Would you like a cup of tea, Mrs. Fleming?"

"Not today thanks, life's such a rush! When do you expect Judy here to give you all her news?"

Annie turned away her head, saying dully, "She's not coming."

"Not coming!" No wonder they were not themselves. "But why? Is anything wrong?"

"No, it's not that. It's just that her mother wants her to go on holiday with them before she goes back to school. Natural enough, I suppose. It's not much fun for a girl to stay here with us when her family's at the seaside."

Morag nearly choked with indignation. What kind of a woman was this to keep the girl away from the old folk who had treated her so generously? Yet there had never been a complaint from the Purdies about their son's second wife. But then, they never spoke ill of anyone. If there was no good to be said, they kept silent.

"Didn't Judy know how much you were looking forward to this visit?"

"Probably she just never thought," was the reply. "I'm sure she wouldn't mean to be unkind."

Perhaps not; but thoughtlessness could give as much hurt as deliberate unkindness. If people would only realise that!

Before she left, Morag took Annie's hand in hers and pressed it warmly.

"I can't tell you how sorry I am you've had this disappointment."

The other summoned up a smile. "You learn to take disappointments, don't you? We're so very fortunate, Willie and I. We've got each other and this nice little house to live in. Think no more about it, Mrs. Fleming. Just you have a good holiday."

But Morag was not the one to 'think no more about it'. She knew that the two had been living for this visit, that in a way it stood for all they had missed in life. They were so undemanding, yet the little they asked for had been snatched from them.

Giving vent to her feelings at night in the Manse, Morag thumped the arm of her chair:

"I'm so angry, Angus! Just blazing!"

Her husband smiled. "Blaze away, dear, it's about all you can do, I'm afraid."

"That's the worst of it. If there was anything I could do, I would."

Her husband did **not doubt** it. Those whom the

world treated unfairly always found a ready champion in his Morag.

In the morning the four of them set off in the car which was 'packed to the gunnels' as Andy put it, with suitcases and holiday gear.

Isabel waved them goodbye. She was going to share a friend's digs in Shelton while they were away. Morag guessed she was looking forward to freedom, and to spending all her off time with Hugh Bennett.

It was a good chance for the engaged couple to get to know each other better. In Isabel's case it was doubly important that she should be acquaint with every facet of the man whom she was going to marry. 'Love is blind' was sometimes a very true saying and once the glamour had worn off a little she might possibly take another, saner look.

As they covered the miles to the port of Ardrossan, Morag could hardly believe she was off the leash at last. Then came the excitement of driving on to the car ferry and at length the arrival at the island. When they sailed into Brodick Bay and she saw spread out before her the familiar scene of Goatfell rearing its head against the sky, and the Castle among the trees, she drew a deep breath of happiness.

Like multitudes of others, the Flemings nearly always chose Arran for holidays. Morag's own island was too far away and there were no relations left there now, but this island was next best.

Their boarding house near Whiting Bay was as welcoming as ever and there was the joy of renewing old acquaintanceships. Morag asked for nothing more than to be free of the need to shop, clean, cook and be for ever answering the door or the telephone. For a time at least she was able to forget that she was the lady of the Manse.

Angus was fond of walking and the boys, of course, escaped to the beach every day. In the evenings they usually went for a run in the car to different parts of the island and sometimes they went off for a whole day picnicking.

On their last full day, Angus took them to a favourite spot called 'The Cleits', where numerous sandy bays lay nestled between spines of rock stretching out to sea. Here one could choose a location and remain there to bask or bathe.

Morag decided to settle down for a nap, Angus read a newspaper and the boys disappeared round the rocks. After a time, however, Andy returned alone, kicking up the sand with a rebellious foot. Morag roused herself to ask:

"Hello, where's Brian?"

"Oh, he's found a girl," muttered her youngest, "they don't want me."

Oh, dear, had Brian got started now. Morag felt a little curious about this girl, for up till now the studious Brian had rather scorned the other sex. She did not have to wait long to have her curiosity satisfied for the pair of them came scrambling round the rocks a few minutes later. The girl picked something from a pool and held it in her hand for Brian to see and Morag heard her laugh. She was a nice, unaffected sort of girl in a blue sun suit and a huge sombrero type of hat which she took off as they talked, shaking out her brown curls as she did so. Morag felt she had seen her somewhere before.

"Her name's Judy," said Andy glumly. "She's picnicking with her folk round the rocks somewhere. Her hat

129

rolled away and Brian picked it up for her. He said, 'Where did you get that hat?' and she told him she had just brought it back from Spain." Morag was wideawake now.

"Judy? What's her second name?"

"How should I know?" And he marched off in the opposite direction, still kicking up the sand.

Angus was lying back with the paper over his face. She touched his shoulder.

"Angus, have a look at that girl down there."

Without moving, "Why?" he demanded.

"Because I'm sure it's Mrs. Purdie's grand-daughter. She did mention she was coming to Arran with her folk. Andy says the name's Judy."

He sat up. "There must be lots of Judys, dear."

"Yes, but not so many just home from abroad. Besides, she's so like the photo I saw. I'm sure it's her. What a strange coincidence. Perhaps it was meant to be."

Angus chuckled. "Oh, come now, Morag, you're talking like Janet Bain. She's always declaring that things were 'meant to be'. Why should it be meant, anyway?"

"So that I can repay my debt of gratitude to old Mrs. Purdie," she replied.

"Well, be careful! That is, if the girl really is the same Judy."

What happened next seemed to be 'meant to be' too. The girl wading at the edge of the water stepped on a sharp shell and began to hop on one foot. Brian took her arm and helped her up to where they were sitting.

"Mummy," he said simply, "Judy's foot is bleeding. Can you do anything?"

"Surely." She smiled at the girl. "Sit down, Judy. I've got some Elastoplast in my bag. Brian, get some fresh water to bathe it, will you?"

"It's not fair on you," said Judy. "You don't even know me."

"Perhaps I do." Morag staunched the blood with a paper tissue. "Is your name Judy Purdie?"

Open-eyed, "How did you know?"

"Your grandmother in Linnbrae is a friend of ours. She showed me your photo. She was expecting a visit from you when you came back from your cruise."

"Yes, I know," said Judy, "but I couldn't manage it. My mother said I'd just be a nuisance to them anyway, with Grandpapa being ill."

As she bathed the cut with the fresh water Brian had brought, Morag went on, "I think I should tell you, Judy, that you would not have been a nuisance at all. In fact, your grandparents were terribly disappointed that you didn't come."

In a tone of surprise, "Were they, really? I never thought of that."

"No, you're young." She applied the dressing to the wound and pressed it firm. "There, that will do till you get home. Will you let me tell you about your grandparents? It's only fair that you should know." And she went on to acquaint the girl with the facts about the old folk, the hard times they had been through, their sacrifices and the dashing of their hopes.

Judy listened, her eyes big with concern.

"I had no idea! They never said a word to me."

"Nor to anybody. They're not the kind to complain, nor to ask for anything that is not freely given. But a small token from you is a big thing to them. That postcard you sent—how proud they are of it. It's on their mantelpiece. They show it to everybody."

"And to think I nearly didn't send one," murmured the

girl, getting to her feet. "Thanks so much for patching me up, and everything. Brian tells me you're going home tomorrow. I wish I'd met you before."

She limped away, assisted very gallantly by Brian, while Andy glowered after them.

With a great effort the four Flemings managed to be among the first to drive on to the car ferry next day. The boys went off to explore while the minister and his wife stood at the rail watching the late arrivals come aboard.

At the last minute two people were seen running down the long pier: a tall man with a suitcase and a girl in an anorak with a big hat slung over her arm.

"It's Judy!" exclaimed Morag.

At the gangway the girl took the suitcase from her companion and gave him a vigorous farewell hug. She waved to him as the steamer moved off and then she turned and saw the Flemings.

"Oh, good, you're here," she greeted them. "I assured Dad you would keep an eye on me. He thinks I'm not capable of getting to Linnbrae on my own."

Morag said happily. "So you're going to pay that visit after all? Good for you, Judy! I hope your parents were quite agreeable."

Judy grinned. "I had to talk them round, of course, especially my mother. But when she saw I was determined, she just had to give in." Her eyes started searching—Morag guessed she was looking for Brian. He was not far away and when he saw who was aboard, he made a beeline towards them. Seeing the disgusted look on Andy's face, Morag could not help feeling sorry for her youngest. However, the day would come for him, too.

They all managed to crowd into the car for the long

drive from Ardrossan. It was a good thing they had a luggage rack on top! The big hat was tied to it as well, for there was no room inside. It was a merry journey; even Andy condescended to join in the fun. To be gloomy for long was not in his nature.

Before reaching the Manse, they stopped at the Purdies' cottage. Judy had gone very quiet.

"Mrs. Fleming, all of a sudden I feel shy," she confessed. "They don't know I'm coming. What if they don't want me after all?"

"No fear of that," declared Morag. "Would you like me to break it to them first?"

"Yes, please."

It was a mission after her own heart. She and Judy got out of the car and Morag knocked at the open door.

"Come right ben," came the familiar request. She went in and there was Mrs. Purdie sitting with an open book which she had been reading to her husband. Her fine old face lit up with pleasure.

"Mrs. Fleming, what a surprise!"

Morag took her hand. "I've got a bigger surprise still. Tell me, just who would you like to see walking in that door?"

An eager light on her face, "You don't mean—Judy?"

At that, Judy herself appeared, her youthful personality bringing a glow into the room.

"It's me," she announced shakily. "How are you, Grandmamma and Grandpapa?"

Morag slipped away without further ado. The happiness on the faces of the two old people was a sight she would never forget.

Invitation to a Wedding

9

It was Sunday morning in the Manse and the Fleming family were getting ready for church. To get themselves out in time with the minister equipped for the pulpit and his wife for playing the organ, everything had to be highly organised.

After breakfast, the minister usually slipped away to his study, while Andy and Brian scrambled for the bathroom and Isabel and her mother coped with the dishes and got the potatoes ready to put on when they got back from church. Crumbs were swept up and furniture hastily dusted. In the bedrooms, beds were 'smoothed up' rather than made properly, though Isabel maintained that the correct method took no longer than the lazy one. But then, everybody didn't have her nurse's training.

They had not long returned from their holiday in Arran and were settling down to 'old clothes and porridge' again. Though life in a country parish like theirs held no great excitements, Morag Fleming was quite happy in her sphere and would have chosen no other. She had begun to suspect, however, that their daughter was not so content with her present lot.

During their absence, Isabel had been living in Shelton with a friend and presumably seeing a lot of her fiancé, Hugh Bennett. Though she greeted the family warmly on their return, Morag noticed a change in her, though it was probably only apparent to a mother's eyes.

Isabel had always been a quiet, self-contained girl, not given to 'tirrivees' as Janet Bain called those shows of temper that the best of young people are prone to. Yet Isabel had given way to quite a few 'tirrivees' since their return, and one of them occurred this morning as they were getting ready for church.

As she seemed tired, Morag had offered to give her breakfast in bed, but Isabel would have none of it.

"You've got quite enough to do without pampering me," she declared. However, she gloomed away during breakfast and was so silent as they washed up that her mother asked:

"Aren't you feeling well, Isabel?"

"I'm perfectly all right," was the short reply.

"Then there's something else wrong. Is it that you're tired of Manse life? Would you rather be on your own in Shelton?"

Isabel lifted a cup and started to dry it, saying slowly:
"Not exactly."

"I know you must find the Manse a bit constricting. Even I find it so at times."

"I don't wonder! You've had twenty years of it. How you've managed to put up with it for so long! All this dressing-up for church and being nice to people when you could see them far enough."

Morag smiled. "It has its compensations, Isabel."

The grey eyes smouldered. "Oh, Mother, I wish you wouldn't be so angelic!" She actually stamped her foot, gripping the cup in her hand so tightly that the handle broke off. Looking at it for a startled moment, she pitched it angrily into the garbage pail.

"There! I've had about enough." And she threw down the dish-towel and disappeared upstairs.

Shaking her head worriedly, Morag finished the dishes and went to get dressed. It did not take long and she was soon down again in her useful pearl-grey summer coat and white hat. Opening the front door to look out, she saw a car coming up the drive. It was a brand new car, bronze coloured and very luxurious. As it slid smoothly to a halt, she saw that the driver was Hugh Bennett.

"Good morning, Mrs. Fleming!"

He got out and with a smile, held out his hand. "Did you enjoy your holiday?"

"Very much," she replied, thinking how handsome he was and envying him the poise which never seemed to desert him. "That's a beautiful car you've got."

"Yes, isn't she a honey? Automatic brakes, a dream to drive. Cost a pretty penny, I can tell you!"

"I believe you." She hadn't seen anything wrong with his old car; it was a lot better than the Manse one. But what did she know about cars? "You're an early visitor," she went on. "Isabel's just getting ready for church."

"Oh, I see."

"Perhaps you would like to come too," she suggested.

Hugh Bennett gave an amused laugh. "Me? I haven't been inside a church for years."

Knowing his views she was not surprised. "Why haven't you?" she asked, straight to the point.

He shrugged good-naturedly. "Got out of the habit, I suppose. Church-goers don't appeal to me."

"Really. Thank you very much."

With compunction—"Oh, dear, what have I said? Of course I have the greatest respect for you and your family, especially the one I'm going to marry. You are exceptions. I meant people like my precious sister-in-law. If that's what religion does to people, I'd rather stay away from it!"

Morag smiled. "I can't say I love your sister-in-law any more than you do, but it wasn't religion that made her like that. I believe, though, that real religion might make her different, if she'd allow it."

"Well, it wouldn't make me any different," was the light reply. "There are many good people, you know, who don't go to church."

"I don't doubt it," said Morag. "But good people who do go to church are better than good people who don't."

He laughed out. "How come?"

"Because, it's so easy to forget to be good, and church reminds you."

His eyes twinkled. "A fair retort. You'd make a splendid debater."

"The world's worst," she laughed. "You'd know that if you'd heard me in that Brains Trust." The memory still made her wince.

By this time she had taken him into the hall. Looking up, they saw Isabel coming downstairs, tall and slim in her summer suit of lime green. Hugh stepped forward eagerly to plant a firm kiss on her lips.

"I've got the new car, darling! Came to take you for a drive."

"Oh," faltered Isabel. "I was going to church."

"I think perhaps you'll be let off for once. That all right, Mrs. Fleming?"

"It's for Isabel to choose," she replied.

"Then of course she'll choose to come with me." He slipped his arm through hers and took her out to view his new possession. It was a car any girl might be proud to ride in and Isabel showed due interest though not, Morag thought, as much enthusiasm as he would have liked. However, she got into the front seat beside him and Morag waved after them as they drove away.

For a few moments she lingered in the drive, reflectively. That car had cost 'a pretty penny'. So had Isabel's engagement ring, she knew. Everything Hugh Bennett bought was costly; he must have a very good income. Still, was it wise to spend so much when he intended to marry and take up house?

Turning away, Morag told herself not to worry; Hugh wasn't a flighty, inexperienced youth. He surely knew what he was doing with his own money. Living on their modest stipend and struggling to make ends meet had made her too anxious about the financial side of things.

But as she played for the hymns during the church service, for once her mind was not on the organ and she made several stupid mistakes. At one point she even went on playing after the hymn was finished! No wonder the choir looked at her reproachfully as the organ tailed off in confusion.

The church activities would soon be in full swing again. Meanwhile, Mrs. Fleming made the best of the late summer days, so still and mellow. Occasionally she would snatch an hour in the afternoon to walk up the hill to the moors and come back with her arms full of heather.

On one of these excursions, she met Mr. Robertson, the blind organist. She was surprised to find him so far from home.

Life in the country and his renewed interest in music had made a tremendous difference to Gavin Robertson. He was so independent now that Ruth was at last going to marry the man who had waited so long for her. The

138

wedding had been fixed for the end of the month in the village church.

The blind man's face lit up when he heard Morag's voice. There was a special affinity between these two who came from the same small island in the Hebrides.

"Mrs. Fleming! I'm delighted to meet you."

She took his arm and turned homeward with him.

"You're looking very well and happy, Mr. Robertson, as if you had found confidence in life again."

"Thanks in the first place to you," he replied. "That day you led me into your church and set me down at the organ was a turning point for me. I enjoyed playing for the services while you were away."

"You'll do it again? Take over the church music altogether perhaps?" she asked. "Now that the congregation knows how the organ should be played, they're not going to be content with my poor efforts."

He promised that he would fill in for her when necessary and in time perhaps relieve her altogether.

"As lady of the Manse, no doubt you have enough to do without that," he added.

"The day's not long enough," she informed him, "and I haven't enough hands and feet, let alone ears to hear."

They talked companionably as they walked down towards the bungalows. Ruth Robertson was at the window looking out for her father, and she came out to the gate to greet them.

"Mrs. Fleming, I've been longing to show you the new bungalow. Can you possibly come in just now?"

Morag could never resist seeing over a new house, so she accepted gladly. While her father was resting in the lounge, Ruth took her into the other rooms which were compact, bright and labour-saving.

"So different from our old house in Shelton," remarked the girl. "Dad loves it here. Our old housekeeper will take care of him when Alan and I are married. It was he who insisted that we put off the wedding no longer. Wasn't it unselfish of him?"

"But you have been unselfish too," was the reply. "You're just getting what you deserve."

In the well-appointed kitchen, Ruth put on the kettle for tea.

"I can't believe the wedding's only three weeks away!" Her eyes were shining. "The invitations are ready to send out, Mrs. Fleming. I hope you'll be able to attend and to come to the reception afterwards in Shelton, with your husband?"

Morag thanked her. "How lovely. I just needed an excuse for a new dress."

"I'd like your daughter to come too. The Flemings have been so good to us."

"I'm sure Isabel will be delighted. She is engaged to be married. Did you know?"

Ruth replied, as she heated the teapot, "I noticed she was wearing a gorgeous ring. Who is her fiancé?"

"His name is Hugh Bennett," Morag told her. "He lives in Shelton; you may have heard of him."

Ruth Robertson put down the teapot with a little click. Though she hid it quickly, Morag caught a look of consternation on her face.

"Hugh Bennett? Yes, I've heard of him. He used to be a neighbour of ours."

"You know him well, then." Morag met her glance steadily.

"I won't pretend we're very happy about this engagement. He's so much older than Isabel, and he's been married before, of course. Miss Robertson—Ruth—I feel I can trust you. Please tell me if there is anything else we ought to know?"

The girl hesitated before replying. "Perhaps I ought not to say it, but Hugh Bennett is quite hopeless where money is concerned."

Morag's heart contracted. "You mean, he's the kind that gets into debt and that sort of thing?"

"Perhaps not now. I hope not. But that was the trouble between him and his wife. They lived from hand to mouth. He had extravagant tastes and used to leave her without money for housekeeping. Oh, there were faults on both sides, but money was the root of the trouble. It so often is in married life, isn't it?"

Morag nodded miserably.

"Now I've upset you," said the other. "I wouldn't worry too much. He may be different now."

Morag doubted it. There was that new car, the ring, other items that bore out what Ruth said. Her thrifty Scots nature had always recoiled from the idea of getting things without paying for them, even hire purchase went against the grain, but she knew there were some people, and charming people at that, who could sail through life and never pay their debts. Was Hugh Bennett like that? Was Isabel letting herself in for a life of misery?

She must warn her immediately. Even though it might cause a family breach, her girl must not be allowed to go into this marriage ignorant of the dangers.

Nothing was said that night, for Isabel was late coming home. Morag decided to speak to her in the morning, for she was not due in hospital till the afternoon. She had not forgotten the stormy scenes previous to her daughter's engagement and knew full well that she would be stirring up more fury. Sorely tempted to let things be, she had to force herself to go up to Isabel's room in the forenoon.

The girl looked round from the mirror where she was brushing her dark hair.

"Hello, Mum! Don't worry about the bed if that's what you came for. I'll make it."

Morag sat down on the ruffled sheets. "Isabel, I've got something serious to say to you."

Impatiently, "Oh, dear, is this another lecture?"

"Not a lecture. Just some truths. Perhaps you know this already, Isabel, but just in case you don't, I'd be wrong not to tell you."

Her daughter sighed. "If it's about Hugh, you can't tell me anything I don't know."

"We'll see." Morag drew a deep breath and went on to give an account of her talk with Ruth Robertson.

Isabel listened, her face hardening. "So that's it. I'm surprised at you, Mum, believing every bit of gossip you hear."

"This wasn't gossip. Ruth isn't that kind of girl. Doesn't it appal you that your fiancé has this kind of reputation?"

"I don't believe he has," was the reply. "But even if it were true once, it isn't any more."

"Are you sure? What about that new car—isn't it more than he can afford?"

Her face flamed. "I wasn't too pleased about that, but Hugh assures me it's all right. Why shouldn't I believe him? Anyhow, he says once we're married he's going to change his ways."

Morag's heart sank still further. "Men have promised such things before. A girl in love always thinks she can change her man, but believe me, dear, it seldom happens."

142

"Well, it's going to happen in this case," was the flat reply. "Really, Mum, you're wasting your time, but while we're at it I might as well tell you something. Hugh has got a shift to London. He's going to the BBC there, and wants me to go with him, so we'll be getting married quite soon."

It was a shock to the woman sitting on the bed. To be engaged was binding enough, but marriage was much more irrevocable.

"You'd be very unwise to do such a thing," she protested. "Please think again."

"We've given it a lot of thought. Hugh isn't getting any younger, you know. There's no reason why he should wait."

"And when you get to London," asked her mother, "where are you going to live? Houses are no easier to get down there than they are here."

Isabel brushed this lightly aside. "We'll get furnished rooms, I suppose."

"It's not the best beginning," Morag pointed out. "A strange place, cut off from all your friends, no house of your own. Are you sure you love Hugh enough?"

She flushed. "Of course I'm sure!"

Morag went over and put her arm round the girl's slim waist. Their two faces were reflected in the mirror—blue eyes and grey eyes, fair hair and dark; unlike yet still resembling each other.

"Isabel, what about your nursing? You haven't got your certificate yet."

The grey eyes flickered, then sparked rebelliously.

"I'm disillusioned with nursing. I want a wider life. London will be wonderful, just what I have always dreamed of!" Her whole being seemed to vibrate with the expectation of a future where she would not be hemmed in or inhibited. Was she looking on marriage as an escape, then, rather than a new, responsible vocation?

Morag replied slowly, "I'm sure your father won't regard this with any more favour than I do, Isabel. It's going to upset him terribly."

"Why should it?" replied the girl. "He knows Hugh is quite capable of looking after me."

But was he? That was the question which haunted Morag during the days which followed. Once or twice she was on the point of divulging this new crisis to her husband, but always she hesitated.

Only after much persuasion had Angus Fleming consented to his daughter's engagement, and the understanding was that there should be no immediate marriage. Though a mild, easy-going man as a rule, he could be stern and adamant when his feelings were roused. If he knew what was afoot there was the certainty of a big family row, with dear knows what repercussions.

So Morag said nothing meantime, trying to pretend that everything was all right, yet knowing that the blow was bound to fall sooner or later. As for Isabel, she went around as if living in a dream, and so the days went on till it came to the date of Ruth Robertson's wedding.

The whole village had been looking forward to the wedding in the little church. It was a gala day for everybody, from the old folk who sat in the back seats and drank in every item for future discussion, to the boys and girls who looked forward to reaping a rich harvest from 'bell money', when the newly weds drove away.

The minister was the first to leave the Manse, while his wife and daughter finished their dressing. When they were ready, Isabel inspected her mother's new ensemble with a critical eye.

"Yes," she observed, "turquoise suits you, though I always think it's a bit ageing."

She herself looked poignantly beautiful in pale pink chiffon with frilly neck and sleeves. Morag's heart went out to her.

"Isabel, dear," she faltered, "about your getting married —you've said nothing more. Are you still of the same mind?"

Isabel looked away. "Of course I am. Why do you ask?"

"I've said nothing to your father yet."

"No, I thought not. Perhaps I ought to tell him myself. Yes, I'll do it tonight, after the wedding. He's got to be made to understand!"

So there was to be no more putting off. The blessed lull was over; soon there would be argument, friction, unhappiness. Once the spark had been lit, where would it end? Morag tried to banish these thoughts as they made their way into the packed church and were shown into the front pews reserved for guests.

It was a scene both solemn and gay. The sun was shining through the stained glass of the arched window behind the pulpit and to add to the colour there were the flowers —roses, dahlias and chrysanthemums, arranged in artistic masses by Mrs. Conway, the flower expert.

The organist from Shelton was playing soft music as they took their seats. Soon the minister himself appeared, to be joined by Alan Watson and his best man, and then the organ broke into the strains of 'Here Comes the Bride'. All eyes were turned to the little procession which proceeded up the aisle, the radiant Ruth, on the arm of

145

her father, followed by the bridesmaid and small train-bearers.

In her rôle of minister's wife, Morag had attended countless weddings, and never once had she failed to be moved by the beauty of the ceremony, the atmosphere of high seriousness and the significance of the vows made by bride and groom. Today as on former occasions, time stood still. A higher presence seemed to be looking on, breathing a benediction, as Ruth and Alan made their solemn promises to each other.

Angus had a beautiful way of conducting the wedding service. His smiling, fatherly manner imparted confidence. To him the words were no mere repetitions but throbbed with new meaning every time he spoke them.

And so, amid a solemn hush, Alan and Ruth made their vows, promising to love and cherish each other 'from this day forward, for better or for worse, for richer for poorer, in sickness and in health, till death us do part'.

Their responses were sure and firm, for there was no doubt in the minds of these two that they were made for each other, and that happiness was bound to result from their union.

Morag was sure of that too, for she knew how their love had already endured under trial. If only she could have felt the same certainty about her own daughter. Isabel had hardly moved during the ceremony, sitting silently beside her mother, as if in a trance. Her mother touched her hand lightly and felt it cold, though it was a warm day. There was no response; it was as if she had been turned to stone.

Then came the happy moment when the couple emerged from the vestry after having signed the register and walked down the aisle arm in arm, a glowing picture.

Morag smiled up at Ruth as she passed and got a smile in return, but Isabel seemed to be dreaming. She was looking down at her hands, lost in thought. Morag had to rouse her when it was time to leave the church.

Cars were waiting at the gate to take the guests to the reception in a Shelton hotel, the Manse car among them. As Morag took Isabel's arm the girl suddenly stiffened, then stopped dead.

"I'm sorry. I can't go to the reception," she said in a choked voice.

"Not go! Are you ill, Isabel?" She had gone very pale and her hands were trembling.

She nodded. "Yes, I—I think I am. Please explain to Daddy and—and everybody. I'm going home. Don't come with me, please, I'll be quite all right."

Breaking away, she ran quickly over the grass towards the Manse. Morag hesitated whether to follow but there was no time, and besides she was not wanted. She got into the car with her husband.

"Where's Isabel?" he asked.

"She had to go home. She seemed to be ill—too much excitement. Don't worry, Angus, it's nothing serious."

But for Morag, the celebrations in the hotel could not be over quickly enough, so anxious was she to be home again. She and Angus only stayed till the bride and groom departed amid showers of confetti, before they took their own leave.

When they got back, the two boys were foraging for a meal in the kitchen.

"Home already!" Andy seemed to be disappointed. "We thought you'd be making a night of it."

Morag asked for Isabel. "She's in her room, I think," said Brian. "She said she didn't want anything to eat.

Weddings don't seem to agree with her."

Knocking softly on her daughter's door, Morag opened it. The gala dress was on the bed and Isabel in her dressing gown was sitting at the window gazing out. She raised startled eyes, haggard and tearful.

"You're back early," she said in a toneless voice.

Her mother replied gently, "I've been so worried about you. Won't you tell me what's wrong?"

The girl smiled tremulously. "I've been having a battle with myself. That wedding ceremony ... Mummy, I hadn't realised what a solemn thing it was, how sacred the promises. It's almost frightening, two people having to keep such vows."

Morag kissed the trembling mouth. "Why 'frightening'? Perfect love casteth out fear."

Suddenly, Isabel buried her face against hers. "That's just it. Is my love for Hugh enough? I've begun to doubt it. We're so different, he and I—our sense of values, I mean. Deep down, I believe in all the things you and Dad stand for, but Hugh believes in nothing. Oh, I know I've been restless, wanting to get away from life in a Manse, but I can't get away from myself and what you and Dad have made me."

"No, of course you can't, dear."

"Marriage is such a leap in the dark," Isabel went on. "You've got to be sure, and I'm not sure, not like Ruth. Oh, what am I going to do?"

Morag took her hands in hers. "If your love is not big enough there is only one thing to do. You must tell Hugh."

"Oh, I can't, I can't! He'll be so hurt. What would happen to him if we broke it off? He needs me, he's always said so."

Morag explained that a marriage founded on anything

but love and mutual confidence was sure to come to grief. Isabel grew very quiet and thoughtful.

"Yes, I know you're right," she said at last. "I know what I ought to do. All I need is the courage to do it."

Morag knew that whatever her girl lacked, it was not courage, and she was proved right. That night, when Hugh Bennett called for her, Isabel and he were left alone. He went away later, stern-faced and unhappy. Morag's motherly instincts melted towards him, but there was nothing she could do. Later, he would find compensation. His was a full life and he would have the distraction of new surroundings. And Isabel?

When Morag went upstairs to bed that night, she lingered for a moment at her daughter's door. Inside, muffled but heart-breaking for all that, she heard the sound of sobbing. Not even a parent could comfort that grief.

Morag put a hand to her heart aching with the pain she knew so well, the pain of a mother suffering for her child. "May a happier day come and come quickly," she prayed as she stole silently away.

The Outcast

10 Isabel's despondency after her break
with Hugh Bennett cast a gloom over the Manse, but life
had to go on and duties be fulfilled. One duty which the
lady of the Manse had gladly taken on was the distribution
of the church magazine. In this way she got to know
people in their own homes and made many friends.

One evening her last call took her down the glen, a
place she loved to visit at this time of year, when the
foliage was rich with autumn tints. The burn sang sweetly
beside her and the mellow notes of evening birdsong lay
softly on the air.

In a wood near the foot of the glen there was a clearing
where Hector Black, a member of the church, owned a
small sawmill. His home was here too, but his wife was
not in, so hearing the hum of the saw, Morag went round
to find Hector, a big bronzed fellow with arms as hefty as
the tree trunks he worked with. He did not see her at first
so she stood there quietly, sniffing in the smell of the
timber and the sharp tang of resin. What a grand occupation his was, so near to nature, so full of simple satisfactions!

He turned and came forward, wiping his hands on his
leather apron.

"Been round at the house, Mrs. Fleming? Sorry the
wife's not in."

"I brought the church magazine," said Morag. "Just

an excuse to visit you in this lovely spot, so out of the world. I don't suppose you get many visitors?"

"Oh, folk come along," he replied. "Some of them not very desirable. My logs keep disappearing."

He indicated a heaped up supply of sawn-up logs which he sold privately and in bulk. "This business just makes me a bare living, you know. Every stolen log means a loss."

"What a shame. Do you suspect anyone in particular?" asked Morag.

He hesitated. "Well, as a matter of fact your son Andy runs around with the young scallywag I suspect."

"You mean Dicky Forbes, I suppose? He gets blamed for everything."

Dicky Forbes was fifteen and had just left school. He was a thorn in the flesh to the people of Linnbrae because of his truancy and wild ways. Morag had always maintained he was not as bad as he was painted; it was a case of 'Give a dog a bad name.' Besides, his home life was against him; cramped conditions, pugnacious, drunken father, nagging mother, and a tribe of younger children who got any attention that was going, leaving Dicky a sort of outcast.

"He hasn't a chance, that boy," she went on. "Which doesn't mean he shouldn't be corrected if he is to blame."

"Exactly. He's never away from the glen, Mrs. Fleming. I've even seen him prowling about at night. It would be an easy thing for him to take the logs and sell them. I think you should warn your son to keep away from him. A bad lot."

Morag had already spoken to Andy, who was quick to defend his friend.

"Dicky wouldn't hurt a fly. Mum. He plunks the school

because he loves the woods. He sits there for hours watching and listening. He couldn't possibly do me any harm."

Morag was inclined to believe him, so did not press the point.

"You won't be taking any action at present?" she asked Hector Black.

"Well, I was going to ask Constable Ferrier to keep an eye on him."

"Don't do it yet," she pled. "If the father saw a policeman about, he'd go for Dicky. I'll have a word with the boy myself."

The other shrugged. "It's not a 'word' that boy needs, it's a skelpit leathering."

Morag smiled sadly. "Dicky's had so many 'skelpit leatherings' they just don't mean a thing to him."

She left Hector Black to go home by a path which led further down the glen and up on the other side. It was like the 'forest primeval' down here: so near human habitation yet so apart it might have been a different world. The green light that shone under the canopy of trees, the soothing ripple of water and the all-pervasive hush gave one a feeling like being in church.

Then to her listening ears came the murmur of voices and through the trees she caught sight of three figures sitting on a fallen tree trunk. Andy and Dicky were carrying on a conversation with the man whom Linnbrae knew as 'Daft Geordie', a kenspeckle figure who lived in a hut nearby. It was a primitive shack of wood and tarpaulin, patched and repatched, and should certainly have been cleared away and its owner sent to an institution long ago. Such was the opinion of a number of Linnbrae folk, but the others said, "Ach, leave old Geordie alone! As long as he's happy and does no harm."

Morag only caught a glimpse of the scarecrow figure before he sensed her presence and, shy as a wild thing, escaped to his hut and shut himself in. Dicky was on his feet too. Thin as a rake with curly red hair and a pale face much freckled, he gave her a glance which was half fearful, half defiant. He was a boy with no trust in anybody.

Andy said calmly, "It's all right, Dicky, my Mum won't eat you. How did you know I was here, Mum?"

"I didn't know, I was just passing. Time you were home, Andy."

"Oh, dear, I'd rather stay here and sleep in the woods with old Geordie. Wouldn't you, Dicky?"

"Ay, sure thing I would," was the fervent response.

"You know, Mum," Andy went on, "folk say that Geordie's just a donnert old man, but it's not true. He's wiser than you or me about birds and beasts and things, isn't he, Dicky?"

"Ay, sure thing he is," agreed the other, his face shining. "Geordie is the greatest."

A strange object for hero worship, reflected Morag; but who could fathom the mind of a boy?

"You going home too?" Andy asked him. "Your mother might be looking for you."

"My mother never looks for me," muttered Dicky. "Naebody does."

As the three of them came back up the glen, Morag questioned Dicky about his future. "Now that you've left school, you'll be getting a job, I suppose. What would you like to do?"

"I'm no heeding about a job," evaded Dicky. "Mooching about in the glen suits me fine."

Andy took him to task. "You can't mooch your life

away, Dicky. Everybody's got to have a job. You could go with the grocer's van or something."

"The grocer wouldna have me," said Dicky and he was probably right.

He came with them to the Manse gate, passing his own house without a glance. It was plain he was not ready to go in to whatever awaited him there. On an impulse Morag asked:

"Would you like to come in and have a bite of supper with us, Dicky?"

He looked astounded. "Me—supper with you?"

"Sure," said Andy. "Is there any ham for a sandwich, Mum?"

Fortunately there was some left on the ham-end which Morag had boiled to make lentil soup. Dicky looked so hungry she gave him some soup as well. The minister showed no surprise at having such a supper guest; stranger people than Dicky had sat at the Manse table and been made welcome.

After supper Morag made a point of getting Dicky alone.

"I was speaking to Mr. Black of the sawmill, Dicky. Now, don't get annoyed. His logs are disappearing and he thinks it may be you. If you tell me it isn't, I'll believe you and he can take his suspicions elsewhere."

The boy's face had flushed crimson. He swallowed nervously, giving her a helpless glance.

"And if it was me?" he asked on the defensive, "whit aboot it?"

"I'd have to tell Mr. Black, of course. But I'd also tell him that if he let you off this time, you would never do it again."

Dicky looked at the ground for a minute, then his eyes met hers.

"All right, it was me. But I'll not do it again, cut my throat I won't." And licking his finger, he drew it across his throat.

"All right, then. I know I can trust you."

Next day she phoned Hector Black, and got his promise that if the thieving stopped he would hold his hand. Morag was relieved. Surely this would be the end of trouble for the boy for the time at least. She must do something about getting him a job to keep him out of mischief.

Alas for her hopes. Hector Black rang up a few days later.

"Bad news for you, Mrs. Fleming. I'm afraid Dicky Forbes has let you down. My logs are still disappearing and I've had to put the matter in the hands of the police."

"Oh, Mr. Black, are you sure Dicky's to blame? He promised me. I was sure I could trust him."

"One can never trust a boy like that," he declared.

"Oh, come, Mr. Black, Dicky's not all that bad."

"That remains to be seen," he replied. "Thank you for taking an interest, Mrs. Fleming. I'm sure you did it for the best."

"Is there nothing more I can do?"

"Nothing, I'm afraid."

Nevertheless, she still hoped. She knew she sometimes erred in putting too much faith in people, but was not that better than too little? She must have a talk with Dicky, get some explanation out of him. She would know if he were speaking the truth.

There was no time to waste, so leaving things in the capable hands of Janet Bain, she made her way to the Forbes' cottage, not expecting to be welcomed. Dicky's parents never came to church though they did send their children to Sunday School, mostly to get them out of the way. If the teaching they got there didn't do them any good, it couldn't do them harm; that was the attitude.

The harassed looking mother opened the door and gave Morag a cold stare.

"Good morning, Mrs. Forbes," said Morag. "I would like to speak to Dicky, please."

"Dicky, him!" snorted the other. "If you ken where he is it's more than I do. He never came home last night. The police have been enquiring too. What has he done, I'd like to know?"

"I hope he hasn't done anything. You've no idea where he might be?"

"Search me," was the reply. "He must have known the police were after him and done a bunk. I can tell you nothing," and she shut the door.

Morag stood, uncertain where to turn. Then she remembered about the glen. The boy might be hiding there, though there was small chance of her finding him if the police could not. However, he was not afraid of her, which was one advantage.

So, down into the green gloom of the glen she went once more taking little bypaths and calling Dicky's name. But she saw no human being whatever, only the creatures who lived in the woods, the wild things that were in many ways like Dicky himself and the old hermit, Geordie.

Geordie. Was that where Dicky had sought refuge—in the hermit's hut? She hurried past the sawmill towards the battered old dwelling among the trees. There she was greeted by a strange sight.

The entrance to the cabin was open and two men were coming out bearing a stretcher. On it lay Geordie, covered by a blanket. His bearded face was still and grey and only the movement of his hand showed there was still life in him. He was trying to wave a farewell.

They bore him up the path towards the road where an ambulance was waiting. Then Dr. Campbell came out of the hut and saw Morag. He asked in surprise:

"Mrs. Fleming, what are you doing here?"

"I came to look for Dicky Forbes."

The doctor glanced round him. "He was here a moment ago. But for him, that old man might have lain here long enough. I gather Dicky found him ill and stayed with him all night. This morning he came up the glen to fetch me. A good thing he did; it's pneumonia. The lad seems to be very fond of him."

"He is," replied Morag. "I think old Geordie gave him something he does not get at home."

The doctor nodded. "I know what you mean. He's going to miss him. Oh, Geordie might get over this bout, but he'll never come back to the glen again."

"Poor Geordie," breathed Morag. "What a way to live! Yet I suppose he was happy in his own way."

Dr. Campbell offered her a lift home in his car, but Morag preferred to stay and have a word with Dicky, wherever he had got to.

An absolute hush descended after the doctor left. A wet mist had come down as if the place were weeping for the man who had gone. Morag crept round the hut, even peeping into its dark interior, but Dicky seemed to have vanished into thin air.

"Dicky!" she called. "Please show yourself. I must speak to you."

Not a sound.

At the back of the cabin there was a large mound covered by a tarpaulin. Thinking the boy might be hiding underneath she lifted up a corner and saw something that made her gasp; a large collection of logs neatly stacked; Hector Black's logs, stolen from the sawmill.

Then Dicky suddenly sprang from nowhere:

"Don't look," he called in a hoarse voice. "You canna look there!" She saw that his eyes were red with weeping and said gently:

"Dicky, it was Geordie who took those logs, not you. Why did you say it was you?"

"Geordie was all right," he panted. "He didna think it was stealing. It was just he felt the cold so much and wanted to keep warm. If they'd found it was him they'd have taken him away. Mrs. Fleming, it doesn't matter what happens to me, but I wanted Geordie to get staying in the glen. It was his home."

He stood there like a timid fawn on the edge of retreat, but Morag put out her hand to him.

"Come, Dicky, tell me all about it."

They sat down on the fallen tree and in little gasping utterances Dicky told her what Geordie had meant to him and how lost he was now that he had gone.

"He was the only friend I had," sobbed the boy. "Now I've got nobody."

She took the rough, freckled hand in hers. "You're wrong, Dicky, you have a Friend who is always near you. He will never desert you and no one can take Him away from you."

He looked at her, puzzled. "I don't know what you mean."

"You used to go to Sunday School. You've heard about Jesus and how He befriends boys like you?"

"Oh, ay," nodded Dicky, "they told us about Jesus right

enough. But He didn't seem real. If He's a friend, why doesn't He show Himself?"

"He does, you know, but the eyes you see Him with are not those eyes in your head. You have a deeper sight than that, Dicky; we all have. It is with this other sight that we see Jesus. He is within us and around us."

The lad listened gravely as she went on, while the silence of the glen brooded over them. "Don't you feel, even now, that there is something unseen round about us, protecting us?"

After a moment, "Ay, I do," he said. "I always feel it in the woods."

"It's the presence of God," she told him. "Often people forget about God. In the past, before Jesus came, they were punished—like Adam and Eve and others we read about in the Old Testament. There was no escaping that punishment for sin. But God is love, Dicky, and He became sorry for the stupid ways of mankind. To save them, He sent His Son to earth with the promise that whoever believed in Him 'should not perish but have everlasting life'."

Dicky said thoughtfully, "That's in the Bible, isn't it?"

"Yes, it's John three and sixteen. Have you got a Bible, Dicky?"

"I had, but the wee ones tore it up."

"I'll give you another. Keep it hidden and the wee ones won't get it. Another promise God made was that His Son Jesus would be a friend to all those who called on Him. He would be there to comfort and console the lonely ones, like you, Dicky. Isn't that a wonderful thought?"

"Ay, so it is," agreed the boy. "But Jesus died. They nailed him to a cross."

"He died to save us from our sins. But the wonderful

thing is that though He died, He still lives."

"It's a bit hard to believe," murmured Dicky, "but I know you wouldn't say it, Mrs. Fleming, if it wasn't true. How could I get Jesus to be my friend?"

"Pray to Him and ask Him to come into your life. Say you are sorry for the wrong things you have done and from now on you will try, with His help, to be good."

The boy looked doubtful. "I don't know how to pray. If you told me what to say—"

To Morag it was a challenge. Was Dicky's case not one for the minister to handle? It would have been easy for her to refer the boy to her husband whose wisdom and faith were so much greater than her own. But she felt that this was a moment which might never come again. Dicky trusted her. He was at the turning of the ways; she was the one to help him and she must do her best.

"Kneel down, then," she bade him softly.

Together they knelt down on the leafy carpet of the wood and as he faltered out his first prayer a hush enfolded them, a beneficent calm like the promise of a new hope for the outcast boy. He turned a shining face to her.

"I think I saw Jesus just now," he said.

She did not doubt it. In matters like these, the simple minds were often the most discerning.

After a silence, "Do you feel better now, Dicky?" she asked.

"Much better, thank you."

"When you get back home to all the troubles there, you may not feel so good. Then is the time to pray again, to keep on praying. It need not be on your knees, it can be anywhere. You'll tell me how you get on?"

"Yes, Mrs. Fleming, if I'm not being a nuisance."

"Never think that," she impressed on him. "Like the

minister, I am here to be consulted. Now, I think we should go and see Mr. Black and tell him about the logs."

After a little persuasion, he consented. Hector Black listened to their story with interest. He was not a hard man and was genuinely fond of the minister and his wife. In fact he was rather touched, as Morag had been, at the thought of the boy taking the blame for something he had not done.

"Well, well," he said to Dicky, "you must have been gey fond of that old man. Funny, I never suspected him, he seemed so harmless. Actually, I'd have given him the logs if he had asked for them. I just never thought."

'Never thought,' reflected Morag, was at the root of a lot of misery. Then she spoke up:

"Dicky's looking for a job, Mr. Black. Have you any use for a boy?"

He gave him a keen scrutiny before replying:

"Well, if you care to tidy yourself up and come back and see me tomorrow at nine sharp, I'll see what can be done."

Next day, Dicky got the job. He was not afraid of work in the woods, his natural habitat. When Morag told her husband about it, he agreed it might make a man of Dicky.

"We'll keep praying for him, Morag."

"Yes, indeed. I believe in praying, Angus," she said earnestly, "but I believe in doing, too."

"I know that, and God bless you for it," said her husband, smiling on her with love.

A Seed by the Wayside

11 IN THE HUSH WHICH FOLLOWED THE ROUSING strains of the 124th Psalm, Angus Fleming gave out his text to the listening congregation. His subject was 'Charity' and his text was from the first Book of Corinthians, the thirteenth chapter.

"Charity suffereth long and is kind; charity envieth not ... is not puffed up ... thinketh no evil ..."

He then began to explain in that kindly manner of his how much happier the world would be if everybody kept in mind those words of St. Paul. His wife in the Manse pew, looking round at all the attentive faces, wondered if they were really listening; or, if they were, would they forget his injunctions the minute they were out of church? She knew the temptation only too well. The world crowded in on you. Good intentions gave way to the demands of everyday living.

Her gaze rested on the face of Clara Rowan who was sitting in the choir. A widow with a newly married son, Clara was a great church worker and made every excuse to call in at the Manse. These visits were a real trial to Morag Fleming, for Clara was a terrible talker and, yes, it must be confessed, her opinions lacked the very charity that the minister was talking about.

There she sat, her small rather shrewish face turned up earnestly towards the pulpit, drinking in every word. Would the sermon have a softening effect on her? Morag

162

wondered. Angus had put a lot of work into his prepara-
tion and the arguments he put forth were sincere and
convincing. Surely he was not speaking in vain!

From Clara Rowan, Mrs. Fleming's glance shifted
instinctively to a pew nearby where Malcolm Rowan was
sitting with his new wife. He was a big, stolid man, the
apple of his mother's eye. The girl beside him, a pretty,
immature lassie with a sweet face, looked less radiantly
happy than she had done a few weeks ago. Morag wondered if it was true that Clara Rowan, who had taken in
the newly weds, was very sore on her daughter-in-law. It
was a difficult position for both of them. Lots of charity
required there.

Guiltily she brought her thoughts back to the sermon.
If the minister's wife didn't pay attention, how could she
expect other people to do it? From then on till he was
finished, she did not allow her eyes to stray from her
husband's face. It was a face she would never get tired of
looking at, though she saw it every day. Quite different
from any other to her, it had what she thought of as a
look of 'holiness' shining through; as if in virtue of his
calling he lived in a higher sphere. And yet, he was not
unpractical, nor too unworldly to recognise the worst as
well as the best in human nature.

Now he was announcing the last hymn 'Be Thou My
Vision'. The organ pealed, choir and congregation sang
as if inspired; it had been a wonderful service. You would
think everybody would go home with elevated thoughts,
too stirred to speak. But as Morag well knew, Linnbrae
could come down to earth with a clatter the moment the
service was over.

Today was no exception. Even before they left the
church, tongues were wagging. Outside, little groups col-

lected and what they discussed was certainly not the sermon. Morag was anxious to get back to the Manse to see about the midday meal, but she was pounced on by the very woman she had been watching in the choir, Clara Rowan. To tear herself away was impossible without being rude, and that would have meant a black mark against her. So she put a good face on it and smiled at the eager little body whose flood of talk almost made her giddy.

"A very fine sermon today, Mrs. Fleming, but of course your husband is always good. So much to the point. I hope certain people I know were listening! The singing was better, too. Perhaps I shouldn't say it, but since Janet Bain left the choir, the tone has greatly improved. I hope when I'm seventy I'll have more sense than to hang on where I'm not wanted."

"Janet loved the choir," said Morag, defending her daily help. "It was only after that last bout of 'flu that her voice really failed. Before that she gave great service. We miss her."

"Yes, surely we do," agreed the other hurriedly. "I've been telling Jenny—Malcolm's wife, you know—that she ought to join the choir. Her voice is nothing special, but she ought to show an interest, don't you think?"

"There's plenty of time," observed Morag. "Jenny is still new to the place. She's got a job, I see, with the grocer. A very pleasant manner, she ought to do well there."

The other went glum. "Pleasant manner, did you say? She doesn't show it to me! And if you ask me, a grocer's counter isn't the place for her. She ought to be at home learning how to cook and housekeep. You wouldn't believe her ignorance! Besides, they don't need extra wages; Malcolm makes enough for both."

Morag cut in with, "I daresay they're anxious to save to get a home of their own."

"There's plenty of room in my house," protested the other. "I like to keep Malcolm under my eye, see that he gets his meals all right. If it was left to that girl, he would starve."

Mrs. Fleming looked round for a way of escape. "Excuse me, Mrs. Rowan, but my husband needs me." And she went to join the minister who was just emerging.

"You do need me, don't you, Angus?" she asked.

"Not particularly at the moment," he replied.

"Well, look as if you do. It's to get away from Clara Rowan."

He quite understood. "That woman has a malicious tongue," his wife went on. "I'm sorry for poor Jenny. As for your sermon, Angus, you might as well not have preached it."

He laughed. "No doubt that applies to most of my sermons. Still, there's always the tiny seed that falls on fertile ground. When I stop believing that, I'll be ready to give up."

She squeezed his arm. He gave such a lot and asked for so little in return. She alone knew how much study and thought, the many hours of labour and soul searching, that went into the short talk which was taken so much for granted by his flock.

A few days later Morag decided to take the bus into Shelton to do some shopping. The bus was moving off as she arrived but the driver stopped for her. Rather breathless she got inside and sat down in an empty seat. Very few people were travelling today and she knew none of them well. However, one figure two seats in front was familiar to her. It was Jenny Rowan, sitting alone at the window with a suitcase beside her. Her head was bowed and her attitude seemed very dejected. In fact, the handkerchief in her hand went up to her eyes repeatedly while Morag watched.

What was Jenny doing here when she ought to have been at her job in the grocer's shop? She couldn't be going on holiday or she wouldn't be crying like that. Perhaps some relation was ill and she was on her way to help. Or, was it possible that she was running away?

Morag considered the girl's difficult position. Married to a mother's darling whom many referred to as a 'big sumph', she simply would have no say in that house. Though Jenny seemed a mild enough girl, Clara Rowan in some of her moods would drive anyone to desperation. It just wasn't possible for Morag Fleming to sit there doing nothing while a fellow human was in distress. She went forward and sat down beside the girl, saying quietly:

"Hello, Jenny! Is anything the matter? Can I help?"

Jenny drew herself away, blew her nose, and replied:

"No, thank you, Mrs. Fleming, I'm perfectly all right."

"Well, you don't look all right. Perhaps you would like to tell me about it. It might do you good."

Jenny sniffed. "I don't see how it could, but if you'd like to know, I'm leaving Linnbrae. I can't stand that mother-in-law of mine another minute."

"I thought it might be like that," said Morag. "But aren't you being a bit hasty? Especially if Malcolm knows nothing about it."

"He knows nothing and he cares nothing," declared the other. "As long as he's got his mother—"

"But I'm sure you're wrong. I know you must find things difficult, Jenny, but if you love your husband—"

"That's finished," the other burst out. "I've stopped lov-

166

ing him. I'm never going back there. His mother and I will never agree. She expects me to knuckle under every time. I've tried, for his sake, but there comes a time—"

She wept afresh and Morag waited before saying gently:

"You're doing this on an impulse, Jenny. Think of how Malcolm will feel tonight when he gets home and finds you gone."

"He's not coming home tonight, he's away on a job and won't be back till tomorrow. I don't care how he feels. Serve him right!"

Morag had every sympathy with the weeping girl. Married life was difficult enough without these added complications.

"Believe me, I feel deeply for you," she said. "I can guess what you have to go through."

Jenny gave a disbelieving laugh. "How can you know anything about it? You're happily married with a lovely husband and a home of your own."

"Yes, indeed," agreed Morag, "but it wasn't always plain sailing. I did have my early married troubles, you know. My husband was an only son, too."

The blue eyes swimming in tears were turned on her. "Really? I'd never have known. You seem to have had it easy all your life."

"We never do know other people, do we?" reflected Mrs. Fleming. "Not really, not what's hidden in their minds. We only see the outside."

The bus was getting near Shelton now. Morag laid her hand on Jenny's. "What about a cup of tea somewhere and then you could come back with me?"

She hesitated. "Well ... No, Mrs. Fleming, what would be the good? Nothing would have changed."

"Yes, it would. You'd have someone to tell things to.

I'm always available at the Manse, Jenny. I'm sure I could help."

They had reached the terminus now and the two got off to stand on the pavement, Morag pleading, Jenny adamant.

"You're very kind, but I've made up my mind."

"But where are you going, Jenny? Didn't you leave word?"

"No, I did not," she declared. "What was the point? I'll write when I get fixed up. As to where I'm going, I don't know yet."

What could Morag do? She couldn't use force, only persuasion, and the girl would not be persuaded.

"I can't stop you, of course," she told her. "Would you like me to tell Mrs. Rowan? She's bound to worry about your disappearance."

Jenny shrugged. "Tell her if you like, but be sure to say I'm not coming back. She'll be glad—" And with that she marched off, case in hand, towards the railway station.

After standing uncertainly for a minute or two, Morag hurried after her to make one more appeal. But the girl was lost in the crowd and even in the station she could not find her. Well, she had done everything she could. After doing her shopping she got the bus back to Linnbrae, not relishing the visit she would have to pay to Malcolm's mother.

She found Clara busy as usual. If ever a woman was houseproud, it was Clara Rowan. She had just washed the front room curtains and was engaged in ironing them. Morag was invited into the kitchen.

"Do you mind if I finish these curtains? They're just nicely damp and will get too dry if I leave them. I thought Jenny would be home in time to help me, but she's late

168

at the shop tonight."

She took a breath to continue her tale but Morag slipped in with, "Clara, Jenny is not at the shop."

Setting down the iron with a click, the other stared at her.

"Not at the shop! What do you mean?"

"She's gone, Clara. I met her on the bus, running away," and the tale came out.

For once, Mrs. Rowan was bereft of speech; but only for a moment.

"You let her go? You knew she was leaving my son for good, and you didn't try to stop her?"

"I did try to stop her," Morag defended herself, "but she was determined."

"Determined, was she? And did she give you any reasons for leaving my Malcolm, a good husband, the best ever, far too good for her!"

"Her reasons were more connected with you than with Malcolm," said Morag dryly. "You can't have been very kind to her, Clara."

"Kind!" Mrs. Rowan began to iron fiercely. "What call had I to be kind? She stole Malcolm's affections, but I did my best to teach her a wife's duties. She didn't want to learn, perhaps it's best she's gone. Good riddance of bad rubbish if you ask me!"

Morag sat down, though she had not been asked. "Clara, you're forgetting how Malcolm is going to feel about this. Don't you want him to be happy? He loves Jenny, otherwise he wouldn't have married her. Granted she's not perfect—who is? But with a little charity from you—"

Clara snorted, laying down the iron again. "Charity! It's time somebody showed some charity to me." Her tongue went on, it was impossible to check the flow; so Morag stopped trying and slipped out almost unnoticed. She was sorry for them all, the runaway wife, the 'sumph' of a husband, and not least for Clara herself.

"Angus," she asked her husband that night after telling him the details, "why do some people make themselves deliberately unhappy by bearing grudges?"

He replied thoughtfully, "I suppose they're happy in their own way, enjoying their resentments."

"It's a poor sort of happiness that creates unhappiness in others."

"Yes, it's what I preach against, Sunday after Sunday. Sometimes I think the Clara Rowans of this world do as much harm as out-and-out scoundrels."

"And nothing one says seems to penetrate," she mused. "I wouldn't like to be the one to break the news to that poor young man when he comes home."

She was to remember these words next day when that very thing was required of her.

In the middle of the forenoon, Morag was surprised to see Dr. Campbell's car coming up the drive and stopping at the door. She was out on the step before he could ring the bell.

"Something wrong, Doctor? Is the minister needed?"

"Not the minister. Yourself," was the reply. "Mrs. Rowan has had an accident. I gather she was hanging curtains and fell off the steps. A neighbour called me. Her leg is badly fractured and she's off in the ambulance to hospital.

"Well!" Morag was quite staggered. The Rowan affair had never been out of her mind since she left Clara last night. "What would you like me to do, Doctor?"

Handing her a key he replied: "I gather Mrs. Rowan

wants you to go along and explain things to her son. He's expected home about seven. You'll know what she means about 'explaining' she said. Is that so?"

"Yes, I know what she means," said Morag, with qualms about the task assigned to her. But, like all the other duties that fell to her lot as minister's wife, it had to be done.

Shortly before seven she left the Manse and made her way to the Rowan's semi-detached villa a short distance away. At the oriel window downstairs one long curtain was missing, telling its own story. She let herself in, glad that she had arrived before the son of the house.

The place was painfully tidy. Every article was in a predestined place and seemed to bear a warning—'Woe betide anyone who shifts me from here!' There was a starchiness about it all that must have been very intimidating to the new bride. And now Malcolm would have to be told the awful facts that not only was his mother in hospital but his bride had fled. What a homecoming!

She ought to have brought Angus with her for support; he was used to breaking bad news to people in the gentlest way possible. How was she going to confront the young man with the truth, see his face change as he learned what had happened? Unable just to stand and wait, she began to lay the table, though she knew he would not eat. Clara's cupboard was meticulous, every dish shining, sugar basin filled, portions of butter and jam ready to put out. She was closing the cupboard door when she heard a sound. A key was turning in the front door. Malcolm had come home.

She drew a long breath, ready to do what had to be done, but the step in the hall was not a man's step. It was quick and light, with the tap of high heels. The kitchen door opened and there stood Jenny, face flushed, eyes questioning.

"Mrs. Fleming!" she looked round. "Where is Malcolm's mother, then?"

Morag explained about the accident. "She'll be in hospital for quite a while, Jenny. Oh, my dear, I'm so glad you came back. What made you?"

The girl sat down, shaken. "You were right, Mrs. Fleming, it was just an impulse that made me run off. When I took time to think, I saw how stupid I'd been. I'd nowhere to go except back to my folk and I was too ashamed. Last night I stayed in an hotel and came to my senses. I remembered your good advice and felt you were my friend. So at last I decided to give things another try. It depends on Malcolm. He isn't home yet? Do you think I should tell him?"

"That's up to you," was the reply. "In any case you'll have to talk things over with him. You'll have plenty of opportunity before his mother gets home. You and he haven't been alone enough to get to know each other. Now's your chance!"

"You're right." Her face glowed with sudden resolution. "I said I'd stopped loving him, but it isn't true! He's my man and I need him."

At that moment Malcolm's step was heard, and he burst into the kitchen. He went straight to his wife and caught her in his arms.

"Jenny," he said, "it's been a long time!" The look on his face convinced Morag that he was deeply in love. Given a chance, such love would surely overcome every obstacle, even the possessiveness of a mother.

She went home leaving Jenny to tell her husband about recent events and to make things right between them. As for making things right with Clara Rowan, that was another problem.

Next day Mrs. Fleming went to see the invalid in hospital. In a ward shared by several others Clara was lying with her eyes closed, a cage under the bedclothes protecting her injured leg. Her face looked very tiny against the pillow and her expression of suffering would have melted a harder heart than Morag's.

The invalid opened her eyes as Morag sat down beside her.

"It's you, Mrs. Fleming—" with a faint smile. "Thank you for coming. Is—is Malcolm home?"

"Yes, he is. He'll be in to see you soon. And what do you think? Jenny has come back."

A slight flush came into the pale cheeks. "Jenny—home?" Then, after a moment's silence, "I'm glad, I really am. Oh I know I said good riddance, but I didn't mean it."

"I knew that all the time," said Morag.

"Lying here in pain with nothing to do," Mrs. Rowan went on, "I've had a chance to think. When I pictured Malcolm coming home and nobody waiting for him. I realised something. Ay, it came to me in a flash that I won't always be here for him. I'm not a young woman and anything might happen to me—like this accident yesterday. Malcolm's the sort of man that would be lost without a woman, he's better with a wife. Mind you—" she rose on her elbow with some of the old rancour— "Jenny is not what I'd have wanted, but he seems to be fond of her and she's better than nobody."

"A lot better. If you're patient, I'm sure you'll find that out."

"Ay," reflected the other. "Patience and that 'charity' you were talking about. It never occurred to me when the minister was preaching that maybe I could be doing with some of it. The cap fits. You can tell him that if you like. I'll try to think better of the lass, see things through her eyes. I can't do more, can I?"

"It's a good beginning," Morag told her. "And here comes Jenny now."

The girl came towards the bed with a hesitating step. "Hello, Mother! How are you feeling?" She bent over to kiss her.

"Not so bad," said Clara. "Good thing you gave up that silly notion you took. Your place is with your husband and don't you forget it."

Jenny flushed. "I'll not forget. I'm sorry about your accident, Mother. Sorry about everything."

"Ah, and well you may be," was the reply. Then, as if it were being forced out of her. "Since you've said it, I'll say it too. I'm sorry."

They smiled at each other, their hands meeting. And so Morag left them. She was well aware that two naturally opposed people saying they were sorry didn't mean that everything would be happy ever after. But at least the situation had been saved, intentions were good, and they had both learned their lesson.

"You were right about that tiny seed," Morag reported to her husband. "It found a bit of fertile ground last Sunday. It may grow up a very frail plant but at least it has taken root!"

Joy in the Morning

12 THE WINTER'S ACTIVITIES HAD SCARCELY
begun before the lady of the Manse realised that things
were crowding in on her even more persistently than last
year. It was always the same. If she managed to shed one
duty, two others were heaped upon her.

The season had started badly. The debt for the dry rot
repairs was still hanging over their heads and the minister
was naturally worried. Andy still showed no signs of picking up at school and Brian, who had so looked forward to
university life, seemed out of his depth. On his visits
home he said little, but Morag guessed he was homesick
in the new environment and had made no friends.

It was Isabel's plight, however, which shed the most
gloom. Hugh Bennett had gone off to London and their
engagement was definitely over. Though Morag was
relieved as regards her daughter's future, the present was
hard to cope with. Life was so empty now for Isabel and
memories so poignant that her nights were sleepless and
her days without joy.

Colds were rife in the village. One morning after Morag
got up she sneezed ten times and knew she was in for it.
Janet Bain was sneezing too when she arrived for her
daily duties. As usual she had a tag for the situation.

"One's a wish, two's a kiss, three's a disappointment,"
she quoted. "Four's a meeting, five's a greeting, six is an
appointment."

"Really," laughed Morag. "And what would ten sneezes mean?"

"That you ought to be in bed," counselled Janet.

Instead, Mrs. Fleming went to get her coat and shopping basket, and set out for the village store. When she had collected all her purchases, which included potatoes, oatmeal and some tinned goods, her basket was no lightweight. Usually it would not have worried her, but her legs were definitely wobbly today and the way home seemed very long.

She was grateful, therefore, when she heard a step behind her and a hand came out to relieve her of her burden. She looked up with a grateful smile into the nice blue eyes of Peter Craig.

"Thank you, Peter, you're a friend in need," Morag told him as they walked along. "I didn't know you were in Linnbrae. Are you on holiday?"

"Not exactly. I've had 'flu, just recovering. Aunt Jean thought a day or two in the country would be good for me."

"She was right. You'll have to come and see us."

"Thank you, Mrs. Fleming." He hesitated before going on, "Is it true that Isabel has broken off her engagement?"

"Quite true, Peter. They weren't really suited, you know."

"I never thought they were. I'm so glad. I expect you have guessed my secret, Mrs. Fleming. Do you think there is any chance for me?"

She wished he had not asked. How could one answer such a question?

"At the moment, I'm afraid not, Peter. I'd wait if I were you, till she has recovered from this—this experience. It has affected her deeply."

"I'm sure of it. I wish there was something I could do."

"Someday, perhaps," she murmured.

They had reached the Manse and she stood above him on the steps as he handed back the basket. His thin face had filled out since last year and he looked more mature, but the fair hair was still bunched boyishly on his forehead. As he passed his hand through it in a familiar gesture, she could see the white scar where the broken vase had cut his brow at the Harvest Festival last year.

"That cut must have gone pretty deep," she observed. "The mark's still there."

"Yes, it's a reminder I never want to lose."

She knew what he meant. Isabel had been the one to attend to his wound. Her fingers had touched his forehead, oh so tenderly, her voice had been gentle and kind. Morag guessed that had been the moment when he fell in love with her. Poor Peter, he must have suffered agonies. And was there really any hope for him? She doubted it, recalling how often Isabel had declared she would never, never consent to be a minister's wife.

"Be at everybody's beck and call, never a moment to call my own? No thank you! I don't know how you put up with it, Mum."

She regarded her mother's position of lady of the Manse as an object lesson, the kind of life to be avoided at all costs. She saw only the drawbacks, not the deep satisfactions and rewards.

No, Peter's prospects were not bright, but she could not bear to tell him so. She took the basket from his hand with renewed words of thanks.

"I'll not ask you in just now as everything is topsy-turvy, but do look in tomorrow afternoon. The minister will be pleased to see you."

She said nothing about Isabel, who had a free week-end before going on night duty. Nevertheless she had a faint hope that perhaps the girl—one never knew—might be pleased to see Peter, and he would help her to forget.

She was due for disappointment. Next day, Saturday, her cold was worse. Isabel noticed it at dinner time when they were doing the dishes.

"I don't like the look of you, Mother Fleming. You ought to be in bed."

"Not at all," was the brisk reply. "I'll work this off, you'll see. As a matter of fact, I was due to visit the Langs yesterday—that cottage away up on the hill. I put it off and must go today, they'll be expecting me. They never see anybody, poor old souls. The fresh air will do me good."

Isabel disagreed. "More likely you'll get a worse chill and be laid up for weeks. Off you go to bed! I'll finish these dishes."

There was a tug of war with the dish-towel till Morag, laughing, let it go. "All right, I'll lie down for a wee while. By the way, I asked Peter Craig to look in today."

Her daughter gave her an accusing look. "Mother! You oughtn't to encourage Peter. If he is coming here, I'm going out."

"Oh, Isabel, the poor boy."

"Poor boy or not, he's got to understand. I feel so embarrassed with him, knowing that you and his aunt are throwing us together. In any case, I was going for a walk. If you like, I'll go and visit the Langs for you."

"The lesser of two evils," said Morag ruefully. "Well, I won't deny it would ease my mind. Take that sponge cake I baked last night, and there's some magazines too; Mrs. Lang likes to follow up the serials. She must have been living in suspense since my last visit!"

She was thankful to get to her bed and ease her aching head. When she came downstairs again, she found Peter in earnest conversation with the minister, but Isabel had not returned. The young man stayed on hopefully, but gave up at last and took his leave.

"I thought Isabel would have been back by this time," said Morag as she saw him off.

Peter smiled gravely. "Don't worry, Mrs. Fleming. I guess she doesn't feel like company just now. I'll bide my time."

She watched him going down the drive, his step more purposeful than dejected. A young man who knew his own mind. He deserved to win.

Isabel appeared shortly afterwards, cheeks pink with the cold air, eyes clear and sparkling. She seemed almost happy.

"It's lovely up on the moor," she said, "and the Langs were delighted to see me. I thought I wouldn't know what to say to them, but it was easy. They're such a genuine old couple! Mr. Lang has some exciting memories of the first war and his wife uses such lovely old Scots words. I've really been educated this afternoon."

Morag was pleased that she had become interested in something outside of herself at last.

"I've promised to go back again," the girl went on. "I think they were glad to have a new audience. They thank you for the cake and the papers, Mum, and hope your cold will soon be better."

Unfortunately the cold got worse, but Morag kept struggling on against all advice. On Wednesday morning when she woke up she told herself she felt better, quite able to go out to the Guild and deliver that talk on the women of the New Testament which she had been preparing.

Her husband, up first, appeared with a cup of tea and she looked up to thank him. But something had happened to her voice. No words came, just a soundless croak. Here was a pretty dilemma! However, she got up as usual to make the breakfast. To Andy it was a huge joke, his mother not being able to speak, but when Isabel came in, tired out with night duty, she expressed concern.

"There, if you'd only nursed it your cold would have been better by now. What are you going to do about the Guild talk?"

Making some husky noises, Morag pointed to her husband, a question in her eyes. He shook his head.

"I'd be only too pleased to do it for you, Morag, but I've got that funeral, remember."

Morag searched her brain. Mrs. Craig could chair the meeting, but to deliver an impromptu talk was quite beyond her. She looked beseechingly at Isabel.

"Me?" said the girl. "I know nothing about New Testament women. I know nothing about anything except nursing."

Her mother nodded encouragingly. "Talk to them about that," she croaked.

"Yes, that's the solution," declared the minister. "Guild women love to hear about hospitals and illnesses. You'd be vastly popular, Isabel!"

At first she would have none of it. She would be far too shy. She had never spoken in public except to address the Sunday School.

"Try it, for your mother's sake," he pled.

As she looked from one to the other, Isabel remembered how forbearing they had been, how her mother's love had never faltered all the time she was being so difficult. Perhaps it was the least she could do.

"All right, I'll try, provided Mum goes back to bed and gets the doctor."

So it was arranged. Janet Bain was left to carry on while Morag gracefully succumbed. Isabel slept all morning and was fresh for her platform debut in the afternoon. Like the visit to the Langs it was easier than she expected. Although all she did was to relate some of her nursing experiences, her audience was enthralled. Morag heard all about it when Jean Craig called in to see her.

"That girl has been hiding her light under a bushel. You'll have to look to your laurels, Morag!"

Morag croaked something in reply.

"Poor thing," remarked her friend, "I couldn't imagine a worse affliction than losing one's voice. Bliss for some husbands of course! Take a good rest while you're about it, dear, it might be long enough before you get another chance!"

Just then Isabel came in with cups of tea for them both, along with some newly baked pancakes.

"Delicious," murmured the visitor. "You'll make a good wife to some happy man, Isabel!"

Isabel was out of the door in two ticks. That was Jean Craig all over. No tact whatsoever.

Mrs. Fleming's cold got better at last, but it had been a bad start to the winter and her usual vim and vigour took a long time to come back. Just when she felt lively again, something would crop up to cause a strain; it was a continual fight. She had never known a time quite like it and concluded she must be growing old and unfit for her job as lady of the Manse.

At last on a day in February a blink of sunshine shone

out on a wet, grey world.

'I'll maybe get through the winter after all,' she thought on the way to the door to collect the mail. Her heart sank when she saw her mother-in-law's writing. Old Mrs. Fleming had not visited them since the day she had come to register her disapproval of Isabel's engagement. They had parted on bad terms and even the news that the engagement was off had scarcely mollified her. She merely wrote to say it was a good thing the girl had seen her mistake before it was too late. 'She ought to have taken my word for it.'

And now this letter, a typical note to say that if it suited Morag she would visit them for a few days the following week, arriving on Wednesday. Morag read it out to Angus at the breakfast table.

"Well, that's very nice," he observed, "I'm glad Mother has decided to let bygones be bygones."

But had she, or would this visit bring new problems? For more than twenty years Morag had tried her hardest to make a friend of Angus's mother, but the old lady had decided at the outset that her son had chosen the wrong kind of wife, and nothing would persuade her otherwise.

Morag was almost afraid to break the news to Janet Bain. Accustomed to get on with the work in her own sweet way, Janet resented the old lady's intrusions and was always in the worst of moods during her stays.

'Wednesday, did you say? Ach well, the sooner she comes the sooner she'll go. Sorry, Mrs. Fleming, I know she's the minister's mother, but we don't see eye to eye and that's flat. She doesn't give you your rightful place for one thing and for two pins I'd tell her so."

"Please don't, Janet. I want her stay to go smoothly. I know it's too soon for spring-cleaning, but perhaps you could put a face on things."

"Oh, aye, I'll do that," she promised, "as long as I get a free hand."

To give her the 'free hand', Morag went upstairs to have a critical look at the spare bedroom, where her worst fears were confirmed. It was terribly shabby, but what could one do to camouflage faded wallpaper, a patchy ceiling and a threadbare carpet? Put in some flowers, an extra rug, shine up the furniture and perhaps cover those streaks on the wall with a picture. She could do no more.

Her reflections were interrupted by the doorbell. The Manse had callers at all hours.

She ran down and opened the door to a lady on the doorstep. She did not at once recognise Mrs. Maxwell of Greenside, for she was dressed very smartly in a completely new outfit and her face was wreathed in smiles. There had been a great change in the woman to whom she had taken a bunch of daffodils last spring. She had proved herself quite human, coming out of her shell and making friends with her neighbours who no longer avoided her.

Morag invited her in. "I won't keep you a minute, Mrs. Fleming. You've listened to nothing but sad stories from me in the past. Well, now I've got something cheerful to tell you."

"How refreshing! I can't wait to hear."

Mrs. Maxwell took the seat offered her. "Since I was left a widow," she went on, "I have never known what it was to have a penny to spare."

"Yes, I know what that means. And now?"

"All that has changed. I've been left a legacy. A cousin in Australia. Quite unexpected!"

"Oh, how lovely." Morag shook her hand warmly. "I'm so glad for you!"

"I knew you would be. I said to myself, you must be the first to know. I only heard yesterday and I went straight up to town and bought this coat and hat, the first new things for years. Do you like them?"

"You look gorgeous. I'd hardly have known you."

Mrs. Maxwell blushed like a girl. "I'm so glad I can share my good news with you. When I was low, you were so kind. Believe me, I'm grateful."

"Please, Mrs. Maxwell, I did nothing." Morag offered her a cup of tea, which was politely refused.

"Another time. I can see you're busy. I'll have a talk with the minister soon."

Morag saw her off, then went upstairs again to ponder all the changes she could make there if a legacy were to come her way. But none ever did or ever would! She had no rich relations and neither had Angus. These exciting things only happened to other folk.

"Now, Morag, 'thou shalt not covet'," she had to remind herself as she took down a colourful landscape from her bedroom wall to cover up the deficiencies in the spare room.

When Wednesday came, Angus took the car into Shelton to meet his mother at the station. She would come on a Wednesday, of course, the day of the Guild. Morag waited at home, if not in fear and trembling at least with some apprehension. She had not slept well and that always made things seem worse. Angus was still worried about the slow progress of the fabric fund. Isabel, though more even tempered, was keeping herself to herself. Andy had spent the whole evening writing punishment lines and there had been no weekly letter from Brian. A fine state of affairs for Grandma Fleming to step into.

At half past twelve the car drove up and the minister's

mother came straight through the house to find Morag in the kitchen stirring the stew.

"I didn't hear you come in, Gran. How are you?"

"I can't grumble. You're looking a bit peaky yourself. And you, Janet," severely addressing Mrs. Bain, at the sink, "still working, I see. Surely it's time you retired."

"I'll never retire," gruffed Janet, who believed in giving as good as she got. "What's seventy? There's older than me still throwing their weight about."

Morag hid a smile at this sly dig at the visitor. Old Mrs. Fleming followed her upstairs remarking, "She's got spirit anyway, I'll say that for her, but you should be firmer with her, Morag."

Her glance went round the room which had been garnished with a big container full of daffodils and greenery.

"Very nice. Where did you learn to arrange flowers like that? Your vases used to be such a hotchpotch."

Never a compliment that wasn't left-handed.

"Mrs. Conway in the church runs flower arrangement classes. I've learned quite a lot from her. I'll have to leave you this afternoon, Gran. It's the Guild meeting."

"But I'll come with you, of course. Are you still president?"

She nodded, her heart sinking. With Gran there, she was sure to be at her worst.

Her mother-in-law then asked, "Shall I be seeing Isabel today?"

"Oh, yes, she'll be home when we get back from the Guild."

"No new attachments?"

"No. I'm afraid she's lost all notion of men."

"A mistake," commented Gran. "I'll have a word with

her about that."

More ructions. This visit was going to be heavy going.

They set off for the hall in the middle of a snow shower. The winter wasn't over after all. While the meeting was gathering Morag introduced her mother-in-law to the people she had not met before, including Mrs. Conway who was complimented very graciously on her gift of flower arranging. No doubt about it, Gran must have been a very successful lady of the Manse in her day, if a bit autocratic!

Mrs. Purdie was new to her, too.

"A good friend as far back as our Briarsford days," said Morag. "It was our first charge and I knew absolutely nothing."

"Well, you know plenty now." The white-haired Mrs. Purdie patted her hand. "You've got a wonderful daughter-in-law, Mrs. Fleming. She's done more for me and my man than I could tell."

Mrs. Craig greeted Gran as an old friend. "So glad you came, Mrs. Fleming. Now you can see for yourself what an efficient president Morag is."

"Indeed," was the dry response. She simply didn't believe it, reflected Morag. Never mind, she had plenty of other supporters among the audience and, fortunately, her bête noire, Sylvia Bennett, was not there to spread any false reports. In fact, Mrs. Bennett had got tired of attending the Guild, as she did of everything, and Morag had made no attempt to get her back. It only took one person like her to spoil the whole atmosphere.

So, trying to forget about her mother-in-law's critical gaze, Morag carried on. The programme took the form of a Bible Quiz in which old Mrs. Fleming joined enthusiastically; in fact she was the only one to gain full

186

marks. A small prize was awarded her and she returned to the Manse in a mellow mood. Morag hoped it would last, but they were greeted by a note from Isabel, left on the hallstand. 'Sorry to be out for Gran, but I've gone up to visit the Langs,' it read.

"What's so special about the Langs?" enquired Gran, not a bit pleased.

"Oh, Isabel has adopted them. They love her visits and she seems to be fond of them. She takes quite an interest in the Church people these days."

"High time she did. Don't the Langs stay up the hill? She's chosen a bad day."

Morag agreed. It was snowing heavily now and the landscape was obscured. While they were still in the hall the bell rang and there was Peter Craig, asking as usual for Isabel. He came at every available opportunity, pursuing a steady if unprogressive courtship. Morag told him Isabel was out visiting.

"I'll go and meet her," he offered eagerly. "Just tell me where."

Giving him directions about the Langs' cottage she advised him to be careful. "It's not very safe up there in this weather. I wish Isabel hadn't gone!"

"Don't worry, I'll take care of her," and he plunged cheerfully back into the snow.

"A fine young man that," commented Gran. "Why doesn't the girl get engaged to him?"

Morag sighed. "She says she doesn't want to marry a minister."

"Why ever not? This modern generation!" It was a constant complaint.

Meanwhile Isabel, having duly paid her visit to the

old couple, turned homewards down the steep path which led to the road. It was difficult going, for by this time the snow was inches deep, hiding the hazards of stones and ruts. It was getting dark, too, and the big flakes blew into her face, blinding her. She staggered along unperturbed, however, till her ankle suddenly turned and down she went, flat on her face.

She lay for a moment getting her breath back, then sat up. It was very uncomfortable here in the wet snow! And her ankle was hurting. Scrambling to her feet she made a grab at the air and promptly sat down again. She must have damaged that ankle pretty badly. Now, what to do? If she continued to sit here she would catch her death. Perhaps the snow would cover her up before anybody found her.

Isabel laughed ruefully. She wasn't seriously worried, yet. After some more attempts she managed to rise and stagger forward for a few steps, then down she went again. At this rate she would never get home.

The next thing she tried was to creep forward on hands and knees, but she was soon soaked to the skin. She thought longingly of the cosy fire at home, the table set for tea and the family round it waiting for her. The darkness closing round her brought a feeling of utter desolation, even fear. She'd better try calling out, even though unlikely to be heard in this lonely, forsaken spot.

"Help! Help!" A thin little sound it was, tossed away by the wind, but unbelievably there came a response.

"Is that you, Isabel?"

"Yes. Yes!" she called thankfully. "It's me. I can't walk!"

Peter appeared out of the gloom so tall and reassuring, that a warm glow shot through her, driving out the chill.

"What's this? Are you hurt?" He bent over her anxiously.

"Sprained my ankle. I've been sitting here for ages. Oh, Peter, I'm glad you came!"

"Yes, it's as well I did," he said matter-of-factly. "I'll have to get you home quick. I'll carry you down to the road."

"You can't," she protested. "I'm too heavy."

"Nonsense. Put your arms round my neck, that's right. Now, hang on. Here goes!"

She clung to him as he walked sure-footed down the treacherous path. Strange emotions were surging through her. She had known he was dependable; she had come to like and trust him more than she would admit, and now that she was in his arms she realised that Peter was no boy, but a man of strength and character. All of a sudden she felt strangely happy. Past miseries counted for nothing. The future shone before her, magically bright.

They reached the road where there was a wooden bench. Peter brushed the snow off it and put her down.

"We'll stop here for a breather."

She laughed shakily. "I should think you need it. Peter, I believe I could walk a bit if I had my ankle bandaged. Have you anything that would do?"

"My raincoat belt," he suggested, taking it off. "It's a good length, and strong."

He knelt in the snow before her and she told him what to do. She looked down at his bowed head, the thick fair hair powdered with snow, and instinctively she put her hand out to smooth it. For a moment he was quite still and motionless then he looked up questioningly into her face.

"Isabel?"

"Yes, Peter."

"Did you mean that? Do you really like me a little?"

A lump in her throat. "More than a little, Peter."

In a moment he was sitting close, his arms round her, cheek against her cold one.

"Darling Isabel. You'll marry me some day?"

"Of course, Peter. Some day."

"That's all I want to know," he said triumphantly.

She limped home clinging to him, rejoicing in his strength and this new, wonderful link between them.

He spoke of the future. "You realise what it will be like married to a minister? It won't be easy."

"I know. I used to vow I'd never be a minister's wife. But lately I've been helping my mother a little and liking it, much to my surprise! Besides, as Mum once told me, love makes all the difference."

"Your mother is a very wise woman," observed Peter.

Morag waited in the Manse with old Mrs. Fleming, wondering when somebody was going to come home for tea. Everything was ready, the table laid, the sausage rolls in the oven, Angus was out visiting and Andy must have missed his bus.

"Don't you have a regular tea hour?" demanded Gran.

"Oh, yes, it's not always like this."

Andy was the first to appear, greeting the visitor with a grin, then turning to his mother.

"Do you know what, Mum?"

She waited, hoping the disclosure would not be too dire.

"The headmaster sent for me to his room."

Oh, dear, couldn't he have told her in private?

"Don't worry, it's nothing bad," he went on. "I wrote an essay about astronauts and he thinks it's good. He says if I go on like this I'll get into a higher class next year. You never know, I might be as good as Brian some day!"

"I'm glad to hear you're mending your ways," commented his grandmother.

Just then Angus appeared looking very pleased with himself. Morag had no time to ask why. Going through to infuse the tea she heard the phone in the hall and went to answer it.

The voice was Brian's. "Is something wrong, Brian?" she asked. "We haven't had a letter."

"I know, Mum—" he sounded quite hearty, "I was waiting for the results of the class exams. I've done well, though I say it myself—" and he told her the particulars. "By the way, you don't need to worry about me being lonely any more. I've got a pal now, a great guy. May I bring him home for the week-end?"

Certainly he could, she said. Really, things seemed to be taking a turn.

Blithely she went back to the room to impart her news.

"I always said Brian would shine at college," said Gran.

The meal was nearly over when Isabel came limping in, followed by Peter. They looked very bedraggled, though strangely happy.

"What happened?" asked Morag, getting to her feet.

"I hurt my foot," said her daughter brightly. "It's nothing, soon be better. Peter carried me."

"Carried you?" Every eye was on them. Morag began to scent something.

"He's very strong," declared Isabel, gazing on him with pride. "Shall we tell them, Peter?"

Peter told them. Congratulations came in a chorus. Gran joined in, too, kissing her grand-daughter.

"So you're going to be a minister's wife after all," she

said. "Well, if you're as good a one as your mother, you'll do well."

Morag nearly fell off her chair at the compliment. "Thanks, but you didn't always think so, Gran."

The old lady chuckled. "Perhaps not, but I seem to hear your praises on every hand. There must be something in it."

Morag and her husband exchanged glances. A quick flicker of his eyelid—could it be a wink?—was accompanied by a mischievous smile.

"I can recommend her myself," he said warmly.

Up in the bedroom, very late, Morag lingered over her hair-brushing.

"What a day! So many good things all at once."

"And here's another," reported her husband. "I saw Mrs. Maxwell this afternoon. You knew she had been left a legacy?"

His wife nodded and he went on, "Well, she's giving a generous portion of it to the church. It will practically clear off that debt."

She gasped. "Then everything is perfect. Oh, Angus, if we could hang on to this moment! I know this state of things can't last. They'll go wrong again all too soon."

He drew her to him. "Of course they will. And then they will improve again in their turn. For that's life. 'Weeping may endure for a night, but joy cometh in the morning!'"

"Oh Angus, I love you very much," she breathed out of a full heart.